Melinda Heads West

Robyn Corum

CRIMSON
ROMANCE
Avon, Massachusetts

This edition published by
Crimson Romance
an imprint of F+W Media, Inc.
10151 Carver Road, Suite 200
Blue Ash, Ohio 45242

www.crimsonromance.com

Copyright © 2012 by Robyn Corum

ISBN 10: 1-4405-5854-X
ISBN 13: 978-1-4405-5854-2
eISBN 10: 1-4405-5855-8
eISBN 13: 978-1-4405-5855-9

Dedication

THIS BOOK IS DEDICATED TO MY CHILDREN, MELANIE, TANNER AND RILEY,
AND TO MY SON-IN-LAW, ART.

I'M SO GLAD GOD GAVE YOU TO ME.

Acknowledgments

They say it takes a village to raise a child. It seems to take at least that to write a book.

I've been blessed with folks who not only read this work in progress, but offered encouragement and praise along the way, deserved or not. Among those who have earned an extra special thank you are my friends, Avril Borthiry and Kim Bussey.

No beginning writer could be blessed with a bigger fan club. Thanks to all for the support. Especially my mom, Judy Shelton, and my hubby and white knight, Reggie Corum. You make my heart smile on a regular basis.

Hugs *and* a one-handed backflip to my dearest cheerleaders: Mary Ponder, Brenda Holsonback, Barbara Dutton, Susan Moore, Dena Nagel, Margaret Suggs, Cindy Davidson and Jan Bailey. You build me up when I am weak and make me think I can climb mountains.

Finally, thanks to my editor, Jennifer Lawler, for taking a chance. Let's hope it pans out.

Chapter One

The stagecoach bumped along the narrow gulch road. Mindy's head and shoulder throbbed from the number of times she'd been slammed against the hard wooden door beside her, but she refused to allow herself to lean against the unwashed, tobacco-stained *person* next to her. Pinching her lips, she straightened in the seat, adjusting the green paisley cotton skirt she wore.

Patience and faith will get you through anything, Mindy reminded herself with a measured breath.

Lifting the oiled leather curtain to peer out the window, she jerked swiftly back, covering her mouth in revulsion. "There's . . . there's . . . " Mindy started, staring at the other passengers in the cramped quarters. She was unlucky enough to be riding along with four unwashed males. Patience and faith . . . patience and faith . . .

"Yeah, we know . . . " said one of the men lazily. "You don't particularly want to look out the coach on that side, ma'am. We're traveling over the Coosa Gully. Nothing but a sheer drop off for about three miles."

Mindy's stomach heaved, and she fought to control it. This task wasn't supposed to be so difficult. All she had to do was pick up a deed to a property. Yes, said property happened to be located three states away from her home in Mississippi. And yes, it was true that she'd never been more than twenty miles away from home before this trip. But it had all sounded so simple!

Yet she'd been poked, prodded, accosted by strange men, lied to, swindled, left by the side of a road only tumbleweeds traveled with any frequency, and had almost been arrested by the crookedest sheriff that ever lived.

If she survived this trip—and that wasn't a certainty—Mindy

vowed she could handle anything else life would throw at her. Certainly though, she soothed herself, the worst was behind her!

That is, if the coach didn't plunge off this rocky path; if she didn't die from the fine stink of her fellow passengers; if she could hold her rolling stomach. There were only thirty-five more miles between her and The Blue Saloon, where the deed awaited; she could hold out that long or die trying. And in that case, Mindy decided, pinching her small lips together tightly, she planned to have her dead body delivered to the saloon, just for spite.

She almost smiled, but then caught one of the men across from her begin to grin back. Shooting him a mean look, she turned away.

*

Mindy had been asleep for some while when the commotion started. The coach was rocking and bouncing like a wild buck.

She jumped in her seat, screaming, thrashing her arms for something to hold on to—oddly enough, the other passengers didn't seem as repugnant now. "Oh, mercy!" Mindy cried. "We've done it! We're goin' over! Do something! Do something!" One hand locked onto the shirt of the man to her left, and she pulled him around to face her. "I'm not gonna die this way, you hear? I ain't ever climbed a tree! I ain't been married! I ain't been kissed!"

Mindy's short life flashed before her eyes, just as she'd always heard happened in moments like these: splashing in the creek as a child, going to church services with her family, disobeying her parents, picking on her little brothers, playing mean tricks on her sisters. Suddenly, she was full of remorse and in the middle of a heartfelt prayer when she heard the man across from her clear his throat a second time.

"Ur, ma'am? Like I say, we've lost a wheel, is all. I reckon you can save them prayers."

Mindy paused, hands uplifted. She opened one eye. Now that

she focused a bit, it was clear that the stagecoach was easing to a controlled stop. Perhaps the driver could be convinced to allow her to stay behind when the coach was repaired. She had managed on her own before, she could do it again.

As the hot, red flames of embarrassment climbed her body, Mindy tried to think back over what she had done, had said, but she couldn't remember. Suffice it to say, the yellow in her had come out waving banners.

"If a single one of you says a word," Mindy said, staring at each man in turn, "I'll scratch your eyes out." She hoped she sounded fierce enough.

Chapter Two

Mindy sat on a blistering rock beneath the only shade to be found, a scrawny little tree that had decided to die long ago, but was taking its time about it. Fanning herself with a limp sheet of newspaper scavenged from the coach, sweat ran from the top of her head to the tip of her toes.

The men had worked on the wheel for hours, it seemed. They had fumed and kicked and fussed and had almost come to blows about the best way to fix the blame thing. Mindy didn't think it was a good sign that they were now sitting together joking and laughing, while the wheel lay forgotten. She struggled to her feet in the heat and walked over to them.

"How much longer 'til we can get going?" she asked, weary of the day, the heat, and even the words it took to speak.

The men grew silent and swapped glances.

After a moment, one stood and removed his cap. Mindy was impressed until she saw the head of hair beneath it. She fairly thought she could see things crawling from where she stood. She took a dainty step backwards.

"Well, therein lies the problem, ma'am, as my ol' preacher used to say. This here wheel can't be fixed. She's had it, that's the plain truth. We're at an impasse."

Mindy raised one eyebrow at his language. "Imm-passs?"

"Oh! I'm sorry, ma'am! I mean to say, we ain't going anywhere in this here stagecoach. Not today." The men beside him grunted and made rude noises. One kicked at the wheel with a worn, brown boot. Dust flew, swirling into the thick air.

"Oh." Mindy gathered her thoughts. A drop of unladylike perspiration traveled down her back. "My."

"Yes, ma'am."

Mindy chewed on her lip. "What is the procedure in a time like this?"

"Well, to tell you the truth, there ain't one. This ain't supposed to happen. But we figured out a plan of sorts. Gibb, there, the driver," the man indicated another individual wearing a tan shirt and dusty brown pants who nodded, "he's gonna take all the horses and go on without us. He'll send back help."

Mindy's eyes grew wide. "You're joking!"

Every cowboy found something interesting to look at. Only one, with black eyes, met her gaze.

The appointed speaker continued. "No, ma'am. That's the only way we can have any hope of getting help. There's not enough horses for the seven of us, and there's a bundle in bank stock and bills up there in that lockbox. Gibb's required to stay with the box. If we send anybody with him, it's a sure bet he'd be risking his life. Money does strange things to the best of people. The only thing for it is to send him by himself, and hope he don't meet anybody on the way."

"Surely I could ride along with him!"

"We gave that some thought, too," the man said, looking around for support. He turned back with a sigh when he saw the others had stony, distant gazes. "But that'd mean Gibb'd be traveling with two treasures, if you catch my meaning, ma'am. Sorry for my implication, ma'am."

"Yes, yes! So what do the rest of us do? Twiddle our thumbs? Recite nursery rhymes?" Mindy's voice rose. "I forgot my knitting!" She was starting to see red—and was becoming a little less fond of the word "ma'am" with every passing moment.

"No, ma'am!" the man replied with a gruff laugh, slapping his hat against a huge thigh. Mindy's teeth grated. "We're goin' to start walkin'. We'll get a good ways before dark, anyhow!"

Mindy stared at the man for a minute. At his happy, hopeful face. She brought her hands around in front of her and clasped them tightly. She took a deep breath and let it out slowly. *Patience . . . and . . . faith . . .*

"I . . . am going back . . . to my rock now. I need to sit a moment," she said slowly. "Excuse me."

"Sure! Sure!" he said as she turned, whipping her skirt. "Don't you worry none. We've still got to get them horses loaded, and get ol' Gibb on his way. We'll let you know when it's time to . . . "

The old cowboy talked louder as she marched away, but Mindy shut him out, seeking the solace of the rock and her shade, such as it was. *Simple!* Why had she ever thought this trip might be simple? Well, *she* was the one who had thought she might want to be left stranded the next time the coach stopped!

Chapter Three

Mindy was rethinking the demand to bring along her traveling bag.

The men outdistanced her with every step, walking singly or in pairs. As a rule, they weren't concerned about her plight—except, that is, for Stanton, the talker. He'd offered his help repeatedly, but pride insisted she refuse it, even though her gait was becoming slower by the moment and her arms felt like they would soon drop from her shoulders onto the hateful rock-strewn road. The black-eyed man up ahead sent an occasional glance back at her, but she felt sure it was in disgust, and that she was becoming more of a laughing stock each moment.

To think that at the time, she'd thought she had packed light! Instead of the two cases, her mother had encouraged her to bring a trunk, for goodness sakes! "Melinda, my dear," she had said, "you never know what company you might find yourself in. The right clothes and accoutrements *do* make a difference."

Even now, Mindy snorted. She knew exactly what her mother had been saying: "Melinda, my dear, you're about to track yourself across three states. If there's a hope this side of heaven that you might meet a man interested in an old maid like yourself, *please* take along enough firepower to catch him!" Well, if "Mr. Right" saw her now, he'd fall off his horse and beg her to shoot him.

Mindy's hair had long since sprung free of the neat bun she'd tried to wrestle it into. She could feel the telltale wisps around her face that signaled an all-out revolt of her hairdo. She didn't need a mirror to know a hazy halo of dark brown curls circled her head. She resisted the natural desire to scream and stomp a foot at Nature's joke at her expense. Her three sisters had lovely hair, perfect hair, well-behaved hair. She had a goat's tail. And she couldn't stomp a foot even if she wanted—her skirt was so weighted down with dust, she could barely drag one leg along with the other!

"Are you sure you don't want me to help you along with that bag, miz McCorkle? I'd be proud to," Stanton said, at her side.

"No!" Mindy snapped, choking back tears. "I mean, no, thank you kindly, Mr. Stanton." The very effort to talk overwhelmed her. Why didn't he leave her alone? The rest of the men did.

The idea of her dresses and underthings falling into men's hands was unbearable. What if her case came open? No, thank you. She'd carry it herself.

Mindy glanced up to suddenly see the black-eyed man charging toward her. His eyebrows had drawn together in a dangerous manner and he looked ready to breathe fire! She stopped in her tracks and, to her shame, shuffled a step so that she was standing behind Stanton when the ogre arrived. Without so much as a word, he reached and tried to jerk the tapestry bag from her hand. There he met resistance.

"*What* are you doing, sir? Those are my private things!"

"I am trying to save this trip from taking three *months* instead of three days!"

"I don't see what my bag has to do with that."

"I can see that you don't, but if you'll give it to me, I'll take care of it for you."

"Oh. Well, that would be kind of you. I didn't realize I was holding everyone up." Mindy reluctantly let go of her bag, glancing at the other men with a small shrug. As soon as the dark man had her case in his hands, he whirled it into the nearby bushes, and then turned to walk away.

"What? How? Are you . . . ?" Mindy stuttered, flabbergasted at the man's behavior. Then she set her jaw, jerked up the hem of her skirt, and marched toward the underbrush to retrieve her property.

"Oh, no you don't, little lady," the stranger said, grabbing her around the waist. Mindy began to kick and swing at him like a she-devil.

He ducked her flailing arms as she yelled. "You better put me down, you heathen! I aim to carry my bag or stay with it!"

"Fine." To her surprise, the man dropped her like a sack of potatoes. "But you'll remember I tried, when you're sitting here at night with the wild animals."

Mindy sat sprawled on the ground in a most unladylike position. Her eyes grew large. "What do I care," she cried, "If the men I travel with are no better?"

The black-eyed man stared deeply into her cold, green eyes until he grew disgusted and stormed off. Mindy rose, dusting off her skirt. Then she calmly started into the tall brambles to fetch her traveling bag. Once again, she was glad she had not brought something larger.

She looked up once as she climbed, very surreptitiously, and saw the men had begun walking without her. She harrumphed and continued her task. She found her bag open, its contents scattered five ways to Sunday. It took her fifteen minutes to put everything back in order because she had to shake off the straw and refold each item. When she came out of the bushes, she was startled to find the black-eyed man waiting on the other side.

"What on earth are you doing here?" she asked. "I assumed you would be off scaring infants by now, or taking food from the homeless."

"Just give me the bag."

Mindy held the bag as close to her heart as possible. "If you think I'll fall for that again, you are sadly mistaken." She sniffed. "There are very important items in here."

"Well, you're not going to need a change of clothes on this trip, *ma'am*."

"For your information, *sir*, there is more than a change of clothing in this bag. There's a gun, for one."

The ogre burst out laughing. "A little thing like you? With a gun? What do you know about shooting? If we left you alone out here, I doubt you'd be able to fend for yourself for thirty minutes.

What have you got, a little pearl-handled ladies' pistol? That doesn't scare away bears or big, bad men, lady."

"I can shoot! Show me a target! I can shoot!" Something about the man made Mindy's pulse pound.

"Forget it. Just give me the bag. I had no idea it contained such important items. I promise I won't chuck it again. At least, not unless you give me reason."

"I'd ask for your word on that, but I don't trust you as far as I can throw you." Mindy tapped one dirty shoe. "Give me something of yours."

"What?"

"Give me something of yours that I can keep in trust."

"You are one unique item."

"You don't know the half of it." Mindy puffed at the hair falling down over her eyes.

The man reached into the back pocket of his jeans and pulled out a leather wallet. He fumbled inside and then drew out a picture. "Here." He handed over a daguerreotype of a stunning woman with upswept brown hair.

"Who is this?" Mindy asked. She couldn't help but admire the lovely woman in the photo. "Why would I take a picture in trust for my bag?"

"It's my wife. It's the only picture I have of her."

Chapter Four

Catching up to the rest of the men, they continued their journey. They walked and walked and walked. They walked up one steep hill and down the next. They walked around sharp, rocky bends. They walked until Mindy thought they would surely walk off the face of the earth— all the while following rugged stage tracks scarred into brown clay.

A vicious sun cared not one whit for their plight and shone brighter than Mindy could ever remember it shining before. The glare hit rocks on the ground and the walls that surrounded them and then burst upwards in spiteful rays of blinding light. The heat was oppressive, pushing down as they walked, so that Mindy felt she not only carried her own weight but the weight of the universe. Gnats swarmed her head and flew into her nose; they raced into her mouth if she dared to open it to speak or breathe.

The party trudged along in silence. Mindy lost her footing, slipped and fell, cut her hands against the piercing stones, and bit her lips to keep from crying out. She wore shoes for traveling, but not this kind.

Mindy's mind wandered. Her thoughts were of home: soft, leafy grass, tall, cool oak trees, and glistening glasses of hand-squeezed lemonade with tiny ice chips. She would have gladly given all the money in her pouch for one sip of that sweet, refreshing liquid. If she listened closely, she could faintly hear her mother calling from the back porch of a familiar weathered house: "Min-DEE!"

How remarkable it was she had dreaded hearing that voice at the time. It had meant putting down the pleasures of play and coming into a shadowy environment where lunch waited. A cool lunch: salad perhaps, just picked from the garden, with crisp greens and bright, fully ripened tomatoes that burst with an ambrosial splendor when you bit down into them. Cornbread with a crunchy, wholesome taste that offset the salad perfectly, and glasses of cool, well water. All she could drink, glasses and glasses, full to the brim and running over, of sweet, sweet, well water.

Thoughts of playing in the stream that ran alongside the house flitted through her mind: wading, splashing, laughing, slopping, spattering. How she had taken that water for granted!

Mindy's eyes searched the road ahead, but all she saw were the backsides of the men and a horizon that stretched into a hazy distance. The twin ruts of the stagecoach went on eternally. How could she have lived in Mississippi all her life and not known about these two furrows that carved their way into an endless forever?

"We'll stop here," one of the men said.

The words didn't filter through to Mindy's thinking parts when they first floated through the air. They traveled around her head like gnats, before buzzing into her ears.

"There's shade for now," he continued, "and the sun'll be setting before long. This is far enough. If I remember right, there's a creek running along the bottom of this hill. We should hit it sometime tomorrow."

Mindy's eyes widened. Stepping dangerously close to the edge of the outcropping, she stared down, searching through the pine and scrub for any hint of the water (water!) mentioned. Her lips burned like they were on fire, and her tongue seemed to have grown to twice its size. Finally, far below, a brown thread could be seen winding enticingly between the trees. With a heavy sigh, Mindy was forced to admit it was much too far to jump.

Instead, with legs of applesauce, she carefully maneuvered to the designated shade and then collapsed into a rumpled heap. There she lay, falling back against the rocks and stones without concern, but registering faintly that there would be new places of pain tomorrow. For now, she didn't care. They had stopped. The walking had ended.

*

Boone sat and leaned against a rock wall. He placed the worn and dusty traveling bag near his side. His arm felt ready to fall off—surely the bag weighed thirty-five pounds! He was exhausted, and the shade felt good.

It had been a hard tramp following the stagecoach path. He glanced over at the girl. She was in a green pile, with brown boots sticking out from beneath a dirty dress. Her hair was a mess, half in a wad on the side of her head, and half running down her back. Though right now, it was all splayed against the ground, and he couldn't remember what color it had been originally.

He had to admit a grudging respect. He'd expected to be slowed by her presence or, worse yet, encumbered by having to take turns carrying her. The woman had surprised him. But there would be no water or food when she awoke, so he fully expected the whining to begin at that time. He'd never met a female yet who didn't pine for attention and special treatment.

Boone momentarily thought about opening the tapestry bag and removing some of the contents while she slept, but . . . he'd made a commitment. And besides, if she found out, he'd never get the picture of his sister back. He smiled faintly, then crossed his arms and closed his eyes, looking for a few minutes' rest.

*

Mindy awoke to a growling in her stomach and a terrific thirst, though, oddly enough, she didn't feel the coarse ground beneath her. She could have been lying on a feather mattress. It was full dark and she could hear the men talking.

" . . . for a woman," one of them was saying.

Stanton's voice was next, speaking low. " . . . worth . . . her salt."

Speak up! Mindy fumed.

"Done . . . well as . . . of the men," he continued. Her pride took a lift.

"It ain't over yet," said another voice. Mindy felt a tightening in her stomach and knew the voice immediately as that of The Tormentor. It rang clear and sharp, and instantly raised her hackles. "We might have made five or six miles this afternoon, but we've got close to thirty more to go. We'll be carrying her before it's over."

Mindy's blood ran hot, and then cold. Her palms fisted and all physical troubles vanished. Why, the no-account simpleton didn't know a thing if he thought she needed to be carried and worried over!

"Forget about the woman," whined another man. "What're we gonna do about food?"

"Yeah. I'm dead beat. I need something to eat and drink."

"Shut up, you two! For the last time!" Mindy heard a sound like a rock hitting hard dirt. Another followed.

"Ow! Whaddya do that for?"

"I'm tired of listening to the two of you complain. We're *all* hungry! We'll stay hungry 'til tomorrow when we get down in the lower region." It was the leader of their small band, though Mindy couldn't remember any decision that had actively made him such.

She sat up slowly. "I have food."

"What?" A chorus of male voices.

"I have food. It's in my traveling bag. I'll be happy to share."

The Tormentor stared. He stood and walked over to her, dropping the heavy bag at her feet.

"Thank you." Mindy said, as coldly as possible. She hadn't forgotten his unflattering statements. She stepped aside a few paces and turned her back. After a bit of fumbling, she unrolled three cans of pork and beans from the clothes inside. She returned to the group and extended them to the man in charge.

"What is *that* supposed to be?" asked the whiner. "I ain't eating nothin' that comes outta no can!"

"Well, I've heard of it, but I ain't never seen it," said another man. "But if there's real food in there, I'll eat the can itself!"

"Hold on," said the leader. "First of all, there's only three cans and there's six of us. We're going to have to split the food, but make sure nobody comes up short." He looked over at the complainer. "If you choose not to eat, that'll just be more for the rest of us."

"Well, hang on a minute. Open it up first, and let me take a look at it."

The whiner rose to a half-kneeling position as the leader of the dusty band took a long knife from a leather sheath strapped near his gun belt. As he carved open the lid to one of the awkward red cans, a rich aroma wafted through the air. Looking up with a slow grin, he dug into the other two, setting each newly opened can on the ground.

The mood in the group distinctly changed, until he punctured the last container and a foul odor jumped out at them. "Whew-ee, boys!" he said, chucking the rank can over the edge of the rock cliff. That means we're down to just two cans."

"Count me out," said the complainer, stalking away from the others. "I told you I wasn't eating nothing outta no can. And you're all crazy if you do!"

"Suit yourself, Byler." As the leader handed the cans around, he made sure to hand one to Mindy first. "Eat your portion and then pass it to your neighbor. I'll do without." No one argued.

Stanton eagerly grasped a can with both hands and gulped down the contents. There was a shout at his side about fairness and eating too much.

Mindy looked at the man standing next to her, solidly built, strong, hearty. She was happy to go first. Tipping the can up, she urged the contents into her waiting mouth. The beans were warm but moist, and filled her mouth with an explosion of sensations. She closed her eyes to enjoy the experience. Her throat welcomed the wetness, her lips gloried in the feel of moisture again. The fact that the dust from her face combined with the pork and beans didn't deter from her enjoyment at all. Her stomach roared loudly and she lifted the can higher, like a babe suckling a bottle.

"Hang on a minute, there. Don't get carried away, you're going to choke yourself."

Mindy wiped one sleeve across her mouth, then spat at the dust. The black-eyed man took the can and downed the rest of the contents.

"Like you care," she said with a snarl. "Then you wouldn't have to carry me *or* my bag."

Chapter Five

The Byler Brothers were getting antsy. It was an easy job: steal the payroll box from the stagecoach and head off into the sunset. But there was one problem. The stagecoach wasn't making its planned appearance.

"You sure you got the right day?" Lee Byler, the eldest, asked his middle brother. Lee was whittling a stick down to a point as they sat sprawled on rocks high on a hill, the afternoon sun beating down on them without mercy.

"Sure I'm sure! How would I mess up something like that?" Ben replied, wiping his face and neck with a dirty, gray bandanna.

Lee stood and paced. He waved the pointed end of the stick within inches of Ben's face. "Same way you messed up that bank robbery in El Dorado! Same way you messed up—"

"Yeah, yeah, I was a kid then. I got it right this time. Sit tight. She'll be coming by. It's just a matter of time."

Lee kicked at a third brother. "Wake him up! He's sleeping again! I swear, one of these days . . . "

Ben shoved at a young, blond boy with the heel of his boot. "Wake up, Roger."

"What is it? Is it the stage?" the boy asked, wiping his eyes.

"Naw. No stage. But lookee here, boys. We do have us some company coming." Lee leaned into a more alert position. By then they could all hear the approaching hoof beats. It sounded like the clattering of multiple riders coming their way, but as the oncoming visitors turned a bend, the boys saw a single rider with several ponies.

"Well, now, Ben," Lee said, relaxing and pulling a pistol from his hip. He checked the rounds. "Does it seem fair to you that that there rider should have four horses when each of us has only one?"

Ben smiled. "Why, no sir! And if there's one thing I've always believed in, it's fairness."

"Then what say we go down and help parcel out those horses a bit more equitably?"

Lee made a motion with the pistol and Ben made his way back down the rocks. He grabbed his younger brother by the shoulder and dragged him along. Lee waited for his siblings to get into position. He loved moments like this. "King of the Mountain" had been a game they'd played as children. One boy would climb to the top of a pile of firewood or rocks, and dare anybody to oust him from the position. What followed was a free-for-all, a throwing, digging, biting, fighting, free-for-all, but the one left standing at the end was the King of the Mountain. The other boys had respected that, and Lee had liked the feeling. He took in a deep breath of mountain air and smiled, then shot his revolver once into the air.

"Morning, neighbor!" he said to the startled rider, who glanced up. The man's ride spooked and reared, while the three horses he was leading pulled in different directions in their attempts to break free. "I'm going to assume you're carrying a weapon, and I'll ask you right nicely to throw it to the side."

As the man began to get his horses under control, he reached for a rifle near his leg. Two guns near him clicked open and prepared to fire. He raised the rifle slowly, staring directly into the hard-set face of Ben Byler. The man had no choice, and tossed his rifle to the ground. Roger ran to pick it up and then to help calm the horses.

"Hey, I know you!" Ben said as he stepped closer to their captive, a man dressed in dirty, tan-colored clothing. He hollered up the mountain, "It's Gibb Tucker. This here's the stagecoach driver!"

"Well, that's right funny," Lee called back, stepping stone by stone down into the tense scene. "You might say we've been waiting on you. But it appears you've lost something. I don't think your boss is going to like you coming in without that fancy box or them paying customers." He grinned at his own humor and Ben laughed out loud.

Lee frowned when the rider didn't cut a smile. His next words turned harsh. "Let go them horses."

The man named Gibb slowly uncoiled several reins from his pommel. "I've heard horse thieving'll get a man killed," he said, handing the lead ropes over to Roger.

"Sometimes a smart mouth'll do the same." Lee's gaze narrowed. "Where's that payroll box?"

Gibb Tucker started to say something, but Roger hollered out, "Here it is!" He'd found it strapped to one of the horses.

"I don't guess today's your lucky day, then, neighbor," Lee said, smiling again. "We hadn't planned to entertain company. But we sure do appreciate you bringing this by to us." Lee glanced over at his siblings; they communicated with a single, decisive look. "Step down off that horse, friend."

Tucker moved slowly. He slid one leg over his mount and eased down into the left stirrup. Then he slapped the horse on the butt, and hauled toward the desert for all he was worth, with himself riding on the low side of the pony.

Two gunshots rang out. The horse stumbled to the dry red earth, collapsing on Gibb and trapping his lower body. "Help me!" Gibb called. "I'm hurt. Help me!"

Lee Byler remained where he was. He clicked open his pistol and spun the chambers in the bright sunlight. He smiled and squinted, showing his teeth and staring at the miniature reflection of himself in the butt of the gun. "Take care of that, Ben. You know I don't like the messy work." Both brothers laughed as Ben stalked off. Lee watched in irritation as his younger brother covered his ears and swiveled away just as a piercing shot silenced Gibb's pleas.

Lee, the oldest brother, leader of the group, coolly reloaded his own weapon. When Roger turned back, Lee was holding the revolver just inches from the boy's face. "Little brother, it's time you decided which side of the gun you'd rather be on." Roger swallowed and nodded, then jerked at the string of horses, leading them past his brother and into the open area.

*

"It's empty!" Ben shouted. He stood over the open payroll box, both feet planted on the dusty red clay.

"What?" Lee marched over to look for himself. "They've sent it some other ways! We've been tricked." He took off his hat and scrubbed his forehead. As he did, he heard a soft moan. Whirling, he marched over to where the man in brown lay dying in the dirt, still captured beneath the huge horse. When he reached him, Lee grabbed Gibb by the collar and jerked him up, shaking him. "Where's the gold? Where's that gold!"

"I don't . . . oooh . . . I don't know." The dying man had bubbles of blood running from his mouth.

"What do you mean you don't know? That's my money!" Lee dropped the man and stepped back. He fired a single shot into the man's arm.

Gibb started to cry. Huge tears made tracks down his dust-covered face. "What're you doing to me? Can't you see I'm already dead? I don't know where . . . " he swallowed heavily, " . . . your gold is . . . but I hope . . . you never . . . find it."

Lee rammed the nozzle of his gun into the man's furrowed, sun browned forehead. "Say that again." Gibb's eyes closed. Lee shoved him harder. "Say that again, I said!"

Ben pulled at his older brother. "He's gone, Lee. Come on. He didn't know nothing. Let's go. We've got to go."

Another shot rang out from Lee's pistol. "I told you to take care of him to start with!" Lee said, turning on Ben. "I didn't mean no gut-shot. Both of you are little children! Next time, I'll leave you home with your Momma."

Both Roger and Ben were silent as they gathered up their own horses and the new ones, and prepared to head out. Lee went to stand on a small rocky outcrop, surveying the area. *I'm King of this Mountain,* he thought. *That's my gold . . . and I aim to find it.*

Chapter Six

Mindy wanted to beg to be carried. With each turn in the rocky road, she prayed for the signal to stop, but none came. She prayed for the call that water had been reached, but none came. Instead, she felt more drained each passing moment beneath the sizzling, scorching sun. Her cheeks burned, her lips were swollen and ached with a fierceness. Her hair hung down in tangled, ratty waves and her hands throbbed from the cuts and bruises she had sustained during her many trips and falls—they cried out with angry voices at the ends of her arms. The dress she wore was filthy and tattered at the hem. And still, the ragged tracks in the ground went on. Her legs now moved independently of thought.

Each time she imagined her endurance had reached its end, the evil-eyed Tormentor cast a glance her way. Her back stiffened and her steps quickened. She would not be considered a hindrance; he'd eat his words.

Her thoughts were as tangled as her hair. Her mind drifted from the present to the past and back again. She remembered arguing with her mother.

"It's not right," her mother had said. "It's simply not done. A young lady does not travel alone. I won't have it!"

They were seated in their comfortable parlor, and to Mindy, the trip had seemed nothing more than a slight inconvenience. She didn't understand her mother's objections.

"Travel is much safer these days, Mother," she had countered. "It's not as if I would be headed into uncharted territory. And who else *is* there? Surely you can't think to take everyone—the cost would be exorbitant, and imagine the younger children on an extended journey!"

Her mother had sighed. "No. That wouldn't do at all. They can barely tolerate a trip to your Aunt Sarah's. Or, should I say, I can barely tolerate them."

"Exactly, Mother. There is no other choice. I'm an intelligent woman, and you've often said that intelligent women can handle anything a man can. Will you deny those words now?"

"Of course not. It's true and you know it."

"Then there's no argument. It's not as if we still live in the dark ages. People travel from one coast to the other with regularity. It's a simple journey. I'll be traveling by train most of the way." She didn't mention to her mother that one leg of the journey would be by stagecoach, no need to have her worrying. Melinda wasn't concerned—she actually bubbled with excitement.

Finally, a chance to leave Rockland and see some other part of the world!

Her mother opened her mouth to speak, but a man's voice came out: "Buzzards."

Mindy was startled from her reverie by the men's conversation.

"Low flying. That's not a good sign." The leader, Lucas, someone had said, stopped and placed one hand to his forehead to block the sun. "Probably just some animal, but it's a bad omen."

"Not far away, neither," another man said.

They didn't walk much farther before they stumbled upon Gibb's body, still pinned under the horse. The birds had done their work and his body was riddled with holes from their sharp beaks, his flesh ripped and torn.

Stanton, walking alongside Mindy, held her back when she would have stepped closer. "You don't want to see that, ma'am. What them buzzards'll do to a creature ain't fit for you to look at."

Mindy turned away in disgust and remorse.

"Gunshot. Hard to tell, but looks like he's been shot three or four times," Lucas said from his position near the body. Mindy's mind raced. What if she had insisted upon riding with the stagecoach driver? Would she be lying alongside him now?

"Horses are nowhere to be seen. I'm sure that whoever did this took 'em. I guess the money's gone too."

"Looks like," said the whining man named Byler. He wore a peculiar smirk.

Lucas looked around at the group of men. "We can't just leave him here. We've got to bury the body. Anybody got suggestions?" It wasn't as if they had tools with them.

The men decided to cover the body with rocks to protect it from the elements. It took all of them working together to lift the horse in order to drag Gibbs' body away.

*

"Water ahead!"

Mindy wanted to drop to the ground with exhausted delight. The sight of the stream, brown and muddy, was like a gift from heaven. She fell at the edge and scooped up handfuls to pour over her head and arms. They ached upon contact, but there was also a delicious pleasure.

Dirty though it was, every person in their party was happy to drink the liquid. Minutes passed in silence while everyone had their fill and splashed water onto red, sunburned limbs.

*

Boone drank until his stomach felt engorged, then sat back and leaned against his long arms. He couldn't quit eying the young woman. He was shocked at how well she had done on the walk. It had been a tortuous journey and would have broken any other woman he knew. But he reminded himself there was a lot more walking to come—she still might fall apart.

He studied her near the stream. He couldn't help thinking that her actions were almost sensual. When he looked around, he saw the rest of the men were watching, too. "All right," he said to all of them. "That's enough. Let's figure out what we're going to do about eating."

Lucas took over from him. "There should be game in these parts. Why don't you and you go down and see what you can come up with for a meal." He indicated a couple of the men, who checked their weapons and headed off.

"The rest of us need to gather wood and start a fire. It will get cooler down here as the sun sets. We'll cook whatever the men bring back." Lucas looked around as if he was checking out the spot they had chosen. Then his eyes came back to Mindy. "You stay here. You've had a tough time of it—just rest up."

*

Mindy wanted to agree but instead her pride stepped up. "I'll gather wood with everyone else."

"Suit yourself, but be sure you go in twos. Why don't you stick with Boone, there?"

Her mouth dropped open as she shot a glance at her Tormentor. He smiled.

"I'd rather . . . "

"Is there a problem?" Lucas asked.

"No." Mindy closed her mouth. She wouldn't create trouble, regardless of the circumstances, but she glared at the dark man, daring him to cause more annoyances. The other men shambled off while Mindy and Boone stared at one another.

The Tormentor stood. "Well, come on then. Let's get going . . . or do you need me to carry you?"

Angrily, Mindy tried to come to her feet but got tangled in the hem of her dress. She spent a moment twisting and pulling her skirt out from under her. She fumed and fussed under her breath.

Boone shook his head and cursed. "I've watched this just about long enough." He crossed the distance between them in a couple of long strides, pulling a knife from his pocket and flipping it open.

Mindy drew back and started to scream just as Boone jerked the hem of her dress out from beneath her. "Stand up," he ordered. Meekly complying, she watched the knife draw closer.

Boone made a cut in the lower part of her dress and then ripped off the bottom foot of material.

"How dare you!" Mindy sputtered.

"I'll tell you how I dare, young lady. I'm tired of watching you fall, and I'm sick of you holding us up. This will make things easier on everyone." He clicked the knife away in one smooth move. "Now come on, let's get that wood."

Chapter Seven

Mindy wouldn't admit it aloud for anything, but the loss of the bottom portion of her thick and dirty skirt had freed her legs considerably. Walking without the heavy encumbrance allowed her more ease of movement and enabled her to keep up with the quick moving man at her side.

She shot him a sidelong glance. He was tall and swarthy, and exuded self-confidence. She bristled. Why did all men think that just because they had been born male it somehow made them more intelligent and important to the world? She huffed.

"Am I going too fast for you?" Boone asked, without slowing his steps through the brush.

"Not at all!"

He grinned and looked at the bottom of her skirt. No doubt taking all the credit for her quickened pace.

"I'm just happy to be off that road and out of the sun." Mindy hopped over a fallen log.

"I suppose so. You are a sight, though."

Mindy stopped. "What exactly do you mean by that?"

"You're a mess. Your face and arms are burned to a fine crisp. Your hair is a rat trap."

Mindy's blood bubbled. "And you think you look better?" She was furious. She was witness to a man who actually *did* look better. The sun had added to his tan and made him look a bit more rugged.

"Maybe not. But I figure you're headed to greet some man. Why else would you be traveling alone? I don't think he'll be too pleased by what he finds at the other end of this trip."

Mindy hauled back to slap him, but Boone easily caught her

arm and pulled her close. His eyes blazed. "Don't start something you can't finish, little lady."

"Oooh, if I only had my gun," Mindy said. "You'd be eating those words."

"Well, you don't." He spun her away. Just like that, he dropped the subject and glanced around. "This looks like a good place to pick up some firewood. Stand still and I'll load you up."

"I'll get my own, thanks."

Mindy selected a spot on the ground and started choosing wood that would be perfect for building and maintaining a fire. She toted branches and twigs from the trees surrounding the two of them to her pile and was idly waiting for her tormenter to say something derogatory about her process or selections when she noticed him bent over to pick up the pile he had collected. She was overcome by an evil impulse and couldn't help herself. Picking up a large branch, she whacked him across the back. He fell to the ground and lay there cursing.

"Oh! I'm so sorry!" Mindy held one hand to her mouth. "Bless your poor heart! Can I help you up?"

The devil eyed her suspiciously. "No, don't touch me."

"I must have picked up a stick that was too big for little ol' me . . . Oops!" Mindy turned to her task again hiding the big smile that bloomed across her face.

They finished gathering the wood in silence and started back to the clearing by the creek. Boone was grumbling under his breath the whole way.

*

As they drew closer to the camping area, Boone suddenly threw his pile down and leapt on Mindy, knocking her to the ground. He brought one big hand around to cover her mouth. Startled, Mindy instinctively went into fight mode, sure that the man had gone crazy and intended to reciprocate for her earlier attack. What he planned to do wasn't clear, but her fears were great. She cried out against his palm, shaking her head and twisting her body beneath his.

"Shut up, woman!" Boone hissed.

Mindy realized that his attention wasn't on her at all. Instead, his gaze was focused into the distance. She craned her head to see what he was looking at, but brush covered the ground around her. As she quieted she could hear the faint sound of men talking.

"I'll let go if you think you can be quiet." At her nod, Boone continued. "You stay here. Do you hear me? Don't move." She nodded once more. She wasn't a fool!

Boone got up on all fours and then to his feet. He crept silently through the woods and Mindy could barely see his backside when he stopped. He listened for a while before backtracking to her.

"It's the men who killed Gibb," he whispered. "They're looking for the money on the stage."

"My bag!"

"Forget your bag!"

At that moment, they heard more voices, and then shots rang out through the forest. Mindy and Boone dropped to their faces on the ground. Mindy covered her head and began to cry. Boone scooted closer and wrapped an arm around her. "Shut up! You'll let 'em know we're here!"

Mindy stifled her crying by shoving a hand into her mouth and biting on it. In a moment, they heard the sound of hoof beats, which gradually grew fainter.

"We have to go check on our men!" Mindy cried.

Boone shook his head. "Not yet. We'll stay here a minute to make sure those thieves don't come back. Then I'll slip up there to check on things and get your bag. Do you have more food in it?"

Melinda sniffed. "Yes."

"We'll need it. I set it down by a tree; maybe they didn't see it.

For now, just get comfortable."

"Well, get off me!"

"Sorry! I was trying to protect you. I forget you can take care of yourself."

Mindy shoved at the man, pushing at his vest. An odd sound resulted, a crinkling, like of paper.

Her eyes widened. "What is that?"

Boone's dark eyes narrowed. "None of your business. And if you know what's good for you, you'll keep your questions to yourself."

"It's the money from the stage! You stole it!"

"You, little lady, need to shut up."

Chapter Eight

Boone watched as Mindy rolled to the side, grasping her legs in her arms and sending him a hooded look. He knew she hadn't trusted him, but figured she hadn't thought of him as "evil" before. Stealing from the stagecoach would certainly put him in that category.

Somehow, he felt a little let down at the idea, but quickly shook off the notion. If the girl thought he was the scum of the earth that was fine by him.

"Stay here," he told her. "I'm going back to check on the campsite."

"I'll do as I please!"

"Suit yourself. But this is a good place to keep from getting killed. I don't think your momma wanted you coming home in parts." He was relieved to see her head drop into her skirts and thought perhaps she'd stay put. But Boone had only taken two steps toward the campsite before hearing her rise. He glanced back. "What do you think you're doing?"

"My momma didn't raise a coward," Mindy said with raised chin. "I'll stay a ways back till we see what's what, but I'm coming." Boone lowered his brows and began to speak, but she quickly added, "You can't stop me."

"Oh, I could stop you. But you're welcome to choose your own misfortune. Now stay behind me and stay quiet. I don't care what you see or hear—you stay quiet! You got it?"

"I'm not a simpleton, Boone. I know people have probably just been killed. I'm not looking to join them."

That answer satisfied him somewhat and he turned, taking off through the brush at a steady pace. Mindy followed more slowly.

Approaching the clearing, Boone squatted near a scrub pine and watched the area for a few minutes. There were two bodies laid out in agonized positions on the ground several feet from each other. It was the men who had gone after food for the rest of the group.

*

Boone studied the scene patiently. Twilight was setting and the darkness would help cover their tracks if the men came back. As much as he hated it, he had the woman to think about now. He wasn't used to considering anyone but himself, and he liked it a lot better that way. He'd be happy when this journey came to an end and he could say he'd seen the last of this particular female creature. She was a burr in his side.

"Did you see the second man over there?"

Boone turned and there was murder in his eyes. "You're a curse, you know that?" he hissed. "It's not the thieves you'll have to worry about if you keep this up!"

Mindy rolled her eyes. Boone felt his blood pressure rise. If they hadn't been striving for silence, he would have shot the woman himself. It encouraged him to think for a minute of other quiet ways of doing away with someone. But then he shook his head, dispelling the sweet visions.

"I want you to stay here by this tree. *Please* continue to make as much noise as you can." Boone said, grinning in spite of himself. She was determined to do the opposite of everything he said, so let the bad guys have her. "Just make sure I'm far enough away first."

Mindy plopped down by the tree trunk and crossed her arms. It appeared she had finally gotten the message. Satisfied, Boone crept off. He didn't look back.

The clearing was silent, except for the sound of the brook babbling by innocently. Both corpses had their eyes open. It appeared neither had seen the end coming. Boone visited each body in turn, closing the eyes and checking the pockets for any important items that might tell who the men were or where to send the personal effects.

"I knew it! You are nothing but a low-down, good-for-nothing chicken thief! As soon as you get a chance you're stealing, and from dead men!"

Boone flipped to his back and jerked his gun out, meeting the angry stare of Melinda, with hands on hips. She reminded him a little of his grade school teacher, who had always believed she knew everything, too. He aimed the gun for the center of her forehead.

"Bang. You're dead," he whispered, then shook his head. "You just don't get it, do you? This ain't a quilting bee, lady. There are real men out there who want to find the money from the stagecoach—"

"Which *you* have!"

" . . . and they are willing to kill to get it."

"Well, then, let's give it to them!"

Boone stood and knocked the dirt off his pants. "Now that's a swell idea! What do you suggest? That we send them a flowery invitation to an afternoon tea here by the creek? Maybe we'll ask them real nicely not to kill us when they're all done!"

"If they only want the money . . . "

"You are a sight! Have you ever been in the real world before? These men aren't like the ones who come to call on you back home, *ma'am*. They are *killers*. They don't care to hear what you've got to say or how your life might be considered valuable to some people back in New York."

"Mississippi."

"Whatever!"

Boone suddenly took stock of his surroundings. "Balls of fire, woman! You've got us both hollering down the heavens. If those men are anywhere close, they know we're here now! You work on me like sandpaper, you know that?" He removed his hat and rubbed his head angrily. "Get your bag!"

"I thought you were going to—"

"I said, get your bag! We've got to go!" Then catching the look on her face, he said, "Don't worry, we won't go too far—there are still two members of our party unaccounted for—Lucas and that Byler fellow. We'll watch from a distance for a while and see if they show up. Since we haven't heard any other gunshots, we should be able to presume they're still alive." Boone turned to go, mumbling under his breath. "But mark my words. Next time, I'll make sure you go with Lucas instead of me!"

Chapter Nine

Twenty minutes later, there was a rustling in the trees on the distant side of the campsite. Boone dropped low, shoved Melinda behind him, and pulled out his revolver.

"Hey! Where is everybody? Hello?" Lucas approached the clearing loaded with firewood. Byler followed him, carrying two small limbs.

Just as the newcomers caught sight of the dead men, Boone stood, still holding his weapon. Lucas dropped the firewood and drew his gun. Byler stepped back. Mindy covered her head.

The two men stared each other down.

"What happened here?" Lucas asked, gesturing with his head to the splayed bodies.

"The thieves, I reckon," Boone answered, unlocking the hammer on his firearm and lowering it slowly. "They came while we were in the woods." He pointed the nose of his gun to the pile of limbs that Lucas had dropped. "I don't suppose we'll be needing that anymore. We can't start a fire and risk them seeing the smoke. Sure as sunshine, they'll be back. We need to get out of here."

Mindy stood and stepped forward. She pointed at Boone. "He's the trouble," she said. "He stol—"

Boone "accidently" bumped into the knee of her back leg, causing Melinda to stop speaking as she tried to catch her fall. Like a gentleman, he leaned down to help her up, turning so the other men couldn't see him. "If you want to learn about real trouble, you just keep talking," he said under his breath. In a normal tone of voice, he said, "Here you go! Upsa daisy!"

Mindy glared at him as he pulled her to her feet.

Lucas asked, "What were you saying? Who's the trouble? Boone?"

"Never mind," Mindy said with a jerk of her skirt.

*

The first thing Lucas did was visit each dead man in turn and go through his pockets. It gratified Boone in some strange way. He knew Mindy was witnessing every move, and he waited to see if she would accuse their leader of robbing the dead.

Mindy watched without saying a word. She obviously assumed Lucas's intentions were good, while his were automatically dishonorable. He shook his head, took off his hat, and rubbed his noggin vigorously. Women.

"This fellow's carrying a bandana with the name 'Rutliff' stitched onto it." Lucas rose and then knelt by the other man. "We can let the marshal know his name when we get to town. This other fellow doesn't have any identification on him, but I'm pretty sure his name was—"

"Stanton, Mack Stanton." Mindy looked at the lifeless body of the man who had walked alongside her for many miles and entertained her with his stories. "His folks are in Bolivar. We should let them know." She turned away.

"Um, yeah. Stanton. That's what I thought. We'll be passing through there sometime, if the good Lord's willing and the creek don't rise."

Byler slapped his leg and laughed. "I haven't heard that old saying in a coon's age!"

Boone and Lucas glared at him. His humor seemed a mite inappropriate given the circumstances, and he quickly wiped the grin from his face. He tried to put on a sad countenance, but it was clear to one and all that he was bubbling with excitement.

"What's with you, Byler?" Lucas asked. "Do you know something about this that the rest of us have missed?"

"Naw! Of course not!" He swallowed loudly, and looked back

and forth between the men. "How would I know anything more than y'all do?"

"I don't know, and that's a fact." Lucas raised his hat and wiped his forehead and neck with a dirty square of fabric. "But you sure act peculiar at times."

Byler laughed out loud. "My momma always says the same thing. I get it from my brothers, I reckon."

"Great. What a blessing to know there's more of you." Boone looked at Lucas and rolled his eyes. "Well, we've got to do something with these bodies. I'm starting to think we ought to go into the undertaking business."

Byler laughed out again. "Hey! That's a funny one, right there! Undertakers! Haw!"

"Tell you what, Byler. Me and Boone here'll take care of these bodies. You go pile that wood up for burning."

Byler shrugged. "Thought you said you didn't want no fire. Didn't want them fellers coming back."

"I don't," Lucas answered. "But I'm tired of looking at your face. I'm getting to where I like you less every minute. Get on with it!"

Byler grunted and went to do as he was told.

Mindy was still turned away. She leaned against a pine tree and sobbed quietly into her hands. Lucas went over and wrapped an arm around her shoulders. "You all right?"

"No. I'm not all right! I've seen three men die in two days!" she cried. "How can I possibly be all right? I planned a sightseeing trip! I had no idea it would turn into . . . into . . . this!" The crying started again and gained in strength.

Lucas tucked her into the crook of his shoulder, murmuring soothing words into her ear. Mindy collapsed against him.

Boone watched them from a few steps away. Comfort her! He'd never even considered it. He turned and slammed his fist into a tree.

Chapter Ten

After another long day of walking, the small group settled down into a secluded area of woods for the night, hoping the trees and shrubs would conceal them from those who might follow.

Mindy shared some beef jerky she carried in her bag. It was the only meal they had.

Afterward, Lucas stretched out his long legs and leaned against a fallen tree. "What I can't understand is why the thieves would trouble themselves with our little campsite. Seems like they woulda taken that money they stole from Gibbs and hightailed it out of here."

"Yeah. Seems that way." Boone was flat on his back studying the stars in the dark sky with his hands resting casually on his stomach. Suddenly, he could feel Mindy's eyes burning into him. *Well, let her stew,* he thought. *I'm sure not going to reveal to the others I'm carrying more than five thousand dollars in stocks and cash.* Boone was a careful man and knew what that kind of money could do to a man's mind—he'd seen it happen too many times. Lucas seemed to be an all right fellow, but his gun said he could get serious when he wanted, and Boone didn't trust the Byler fellow as far as a flying chicken!

To her credit, Mindy said nothing. Evidently the warning he'd given her earlier had stung. *Good. Might keep her out of trouble for a change.*

Rolling his head so he could see her, Boone couldn't help but grin. She was sitting against a tree, messing with her hair, though it was to no profit. She looked like death on a cracker.

"You think that's going to help?" he asked.

"Shut up," she replied as she continued her task, determined to will the mass of unruly strands back into a knot on the back of her head. Having lost most of her hairpins along the way didn't help. Finally, she gave out a tremendous sigh and a grunt and gave up.

Boone looked closer. Melinda's face was blistering and there were signs it was beginning to peel around the edges of her hairline and on her nose.

"You'll need to put mud on your face tomorrow before we head out."

"Pardon me?"

"Mud. It'll keep the sun off somewhat."

"Oh, you'd like that, wouldn't you? Give yourself one more thing to laugh about?" Mindy frowned, grabbed a nearby rock, and threw it at him.

"No, he's right," Lucas interjected. "You're red as a tomato. The mud will help some."

"Oh." Mindy was quiet a moment, but when she caught Boone looking at her, she made a face and stuck out her tongue.

Boone laughed again. "You'll need to put some on your legs as well. I suppose they aren't used to seeing much daylight."

"You're a pig, do you know that?" Mindy said. "How on earth you ever got a wife is beyond me." She crossed her arms and looked to the side.

Boone tensed. "Don't you mind about my wife! She's none of your business and I'll thank you to keep your mouth shut about her."

Mindy snorted.

Boone crossed his arms and closed his eyes, determined to will himself to sleep. Before he could help himself, he spoke again. "It might surprise you to know she thinks I'm a fine fellow."

"You must stay on the road a lot. Or you're just fooling yourself. Or she's blind and deaf!"

Boone sat up, sparks flying from his eyes. "My wife worships me! We're extremely happy with our home and three little children." He didn't understand why these words were coming out of his mouth. The "wife" she referred to was his sister, from the picture he'd allowed her to hold, and there were no children.

Somehow this tiny lady brought out the rooster in him. He was crowing like mad!

Mindy leaned forward. "Ha! See if she's home when you get back. I'll bet—"

"All right, that's enough! You two act like brother and sister the way you go at each other."

"Humphf! If he was my brother, I would have already—"

"Already what? I'm real interested to know just what you think you would have done!"

"Never mind! Leave me alone!"

"Yeah, leave off, Boone. You're being a little rough," Lucas said.

"*Me*? She started it! I was trying to help her out with the mud!"

"Just shut up, both of you!" Lucas shouted, staring the squabblers down. They grew quiet. "Get some sleep. Tomorrow will be another long day."

Boone shot Mindy another venomous glare before he lay back down and rolled to his side. He propped one arm beneath his head. "Women!"

Chapter Eleven

The travelers awoke to the click of hammers. Surrounding them were three unruly looking gentlemen with amused looks.

"Why, lookee here what we done found, brothers! A party! And us without an in—*vi*—tation," a stranger with cold eyes said, throwing a cocky look over a shoulder to his two companions.

"You think maybe they'll allow us to come late?" A second man said with a chuckle, until he saw the look in his compatriot's eye. For some reason, his laugh cut off uncomfortably in the middle. "Sorry, Lee."

"Well, now. that's all right! It just might be that these nice folks will let us join their party. You might say we brought the entertainment."

The two other men bearing guns grinned and nodded.

"Who are you and what do you want?" Lucas asked.

The man named Lee ignored him and stepped closer to one of the people on the ground. The traveler called Byler was lounging casually with one elbow propped beneath him. He grinned at the man holding the gun. "It's good to see you, brother. I wondered when you would get here."

Mindy drew back in horror, putting one hand to her mouth, as she realized she'd spent the last few days traveling with a potential thief and murderer. Boone motioned for her to remain calm.

Lucas regarded the group of dirty thieves with disgust. "I don't like repeating myself, but who are you and what do you want?" he said, a little more forcefully.

"Now, I'm glad you asked that, friend. See, there's this matter of some gold, missing from the stagecoach. As far as I'm concerned, that's my gold. I am headstrong on finding it." Lee Byler wore a wide smile.

"What gold?" Lucas replied. "We don't have your money. Gibb

had it—the coach driver. Somebody killed him and took it. Go look for them."

"That's where you're wrong, neighbor. We happened to be there when ol' Gibb had his 'accident.' That cashbox was empty. I figure one of you four either has the money or knows where it is. So we're going to have a discussion. Now, throw me your guns."

Lucas and Boone withdrew their weapons and tossed them toward Lee. A younger brother scurried to pick them up and then chucked them in the muddy stream.

There was a long pause. Lee Byler seemed to enjoy the silence and allowed it to draw out. Mindy had pulled herself into a ball beside a tree and Boone was slowly easing toward her. Lucas tried to stare Lee down.

"So, where's the gold?" the middle brother finally shouted. "We don't plan to stand around all day."

"My brother's right, for once. Someone speak up." He pointed the tip of his gun toward Boone. "Stay right where you are. When people move around too much, Ben here gets a little antsy. His gun's got a feather trigger and I wouldn't test it if I were you."

Boone glanced over to Mindy. "Are you all right?" his eyes seemed to ask. She nodded nervously.

Lee looked over to the man they knew as Byler, who was calmly watching the proceedings. "You know anything, Rich?"

"Not a thing, brother."

"Fat lot of good you've been." Lee snarled. "I ought to kill you with the rest of 'em."

"I know where the money is," Mindy interjected. "If you promise not to kill anyone, I'll tell you."

Lee turned his head in her direction and raised an eyebrow. He smiled at each of his brothers in turn and then stepped over to where Mindy sat with her arms wrapped tightly around her knees. He squatted and put his gun within inches of her nose. "Oh, I promise, and I'm a gentleman of the best sort."

She nodded her head in Boone's direction. "Boone—"

At that moment, the world turned upside down. Lucas lunged onto Rich Byler, whose holster was riding high on his right hip as he lounged on the ground. Lucas bent the gun belt up and fired off two shots in quick order. The middle Byler brother, Ben, and the youngest one, Roger, hit the ground. As Lucas tried to twist the gun toward Lee, Rich rolled away. Lee fired off one shot before Boone was on him, knocking Lee to the ground and wrestling him for the gun. Mindy covered her head and screamed.

It was over in a moment. Boone stood panting over Lee, pointing the gun down at him.

"Look out!" Mindy hollered. Boone whirled to his left, just as a bullet whizzed by his ear. Rich lay on the ground, firing. The sibling pulled the trigger again, but the gun only clicked. Boone fired back and Byler's gun hand went limp. He hunched over, crying.

Lee Byler used the distraction to knock Boone's legs out from under him. When he hit the ground, the gun went flying, landing in brambles beyond Mindy.

Boone and Lee jumped each other and fought like animals, pounding and pummeling. When Lee pulled out a knife, Boone scooted backwards.

Lee rose to his feet and motioned for Rich to stand as well. He glanced over his shoulder at the other two brothers who lay motionless on the soft grass. "I think that's about enough." He wiped blood from one corner of his mouth. "I don't like it too much when things don't go as I plan." He looked over to Rich again. "Get up! You lazy coward!"

"But my hand's been shot off, Lee," Byler moaned.

"It's barely shot at all! Get up and help me. You can wrap it later!"

Rich staggered to his feet, holding one bloody hand to his stomach.

"Get some rope!"

"Yes, sir." Rich hobbled over to the horses; there were seven tied to a tree not far from the campsite.

No one had been watching Mindy. She had inched over to her bag, reached in and fumbled for her gun, pulling out a heavy fifteen-inch-long revolver. She raised the weapon and aimed directly for Lee Byler.

"I think you should be still." There was only a small tremble in her voice. "Throw down that knife. Don't make me shoot. I've never shot a man before."

Lee Byler laughed and took a couple of steps toward her. "It don't look like you've ever shot at all, girlie. Leave this to the men and hand over that gun." Mindy came to her feet, sliding one hand up the tree. "I'll thank you to know I'm a good shot! Now be smart and don't try me and you won't have to find out."

Byler lowered the knife and tossed it to the side. Boone grabbed the gun from Mindy and pointed it so that both brothers were covered. "It's time for you two to get on out of here. While there's still some of you left."

Lee gestured to Rich, who made a move to gather the horses.

"Leave the horses! Just get out of here."

The brothers had no choice and turned, heading off the way they had come. Boone watched until he was sure they were gone.

Mindy turned back to the campsite and then screamed. She jerked up her skirt and dashed to Lucas's side. "Boone!" she screamed again, as she kneeled over the prone man. "He's been shot!"

Chapter Twelve

Boone ran over to Lucas and Mindy. His first sight of the large, blond-headed man had him thinking the worst, but then Lucas groaned. Boone shoved Mindy backwards to get a better look at the wound. "Howya doin' soldier?"

It took a moment for Lucas to reply. "Hurting . . . " His silk shirt had a quarter-sized hole in the right side of the chest. Blood was quickly saturating the garment.

"I guess so—they shot the dickens out of you. Hang on, though, you're not dead yet."

Mindy had been watching. Now she pushed Boone aside and straddled Lucas, pressing hard on his chest with both hands.

Lucas groaned.

"What do you think you're doing? He's hurting bad enough as it is!"

"Shut up! I'm trying to stop the bleeding. Go get my bag. Now!"

Boone, shocked by her demeanor, rose to do what she asked. He placed the bag near where her small frame was centered on top of Lucas's chest. Her orders were brisk. "Go start a fire and boil me some horsehair." Boone looked at her in surprise. Her eyes flickered with anger. "Would you just do it?"

Boone set about grabbing branches and twigs and making the fire. As he waited for it to burn brighter, he ran to the horses and was back in a flash. The fire was burning strong. "What am I supposed to boil the water in?"

"There's a cup in my bag. Now, take off your hat and bring me some water to wash my hands." Boone did as he was told. "Here, I'm going to let up this pressure, but you take over." Mindy eased her hands off Lucas's wound and Boone shoved hard. Lucas grunted again.

"Sorry, brother. I'm just following doctor's orders. Hang in there. I think she knows what she's doing."

"No, I don't," Mindy said, looking into Boone's eyes. "I've never dealt with a gunshot wound before. My brothers have pulled plenty of awful stunts in their lives, but nothing this bad."

"I got faith in you," he replied. And he did.

After rinsing her hands, Melinda dug in her bag and pulled out a tin cup and a sewing kit. She looked up at Boone. "I need your knife."

Boone dug one bloody hand deep in his pocket and pulled out a folded blade. He handed it over. Mindy took the knife and rinsed it off in the water still left in the hat. Then she took a deep breath and ordered Boone away from Lucas.

She eased his shirt away from the wound. "Thank goodness," she said. "The shirt is still intact." She looked up at Boone with a relieved sigh. "It didn't pull off in him." She laughed a little and shook her head. "Lucas, you are one lucky man."

"That's why . . . I wear silk . . . now." Lucas laughed lightly. In between words, he ground his teeth. "Saw too . . . many die in the war from . . . infection."

"Well, turns out you're a smart man. A real smart man. You're doing good. We've got the bleeding stopped now."

"My angel . . . of mercy."

"Shut that up. I'm no angel, that's for sure. And as far as mercy is concerned, I'd say a prayer for some of that, if I was you."

"Never been . . . a praying man," Lucas grunted. His body began to shake.

Melinda dashed tears from her eyes with the back of one hand. "This would be a good time to start. Before I do what I'm gonna have to do."

Lucas turned his head so he could see Melinda more clearly. "It's okay. I trust you."

Mindy sat back on her heels. She took another deep breath in and out. "My momma always said if a person could last thirty seconds with a bad wound, he was more likely to last thirty minutes. If he lasted thirty minutes, he was liable to last three hours. Three hours equals three days. And so on. You're almost to thirty minutes, I'd guess. If I don't kill you, you got a little time left to learn how to pray."

Lucas chuckled and relaxed his head. Boone sat near the small woman, watching her efficient movements. She turned to him. "You're gonna have to lie over him. This won't be easy."

Boone stretched out across Lucas's legs and hips, positioned so that he could see her work. He was amazed. He'd never seen a woman hold up so well in the face of disaster, much less be willing to dig in and do something about it. Well, except his mother.

Mindy waited until Lucas was secure. "You're going to have to stop that shivering, Lucas! I can't do a thing while you're moving around like that!" Lucas's face grew red with the effort, but his body stopped moving. Blood started to rise up in the wound. Regardless, Mindy leaned over Lucas with the knife and started probing delicately. Boone looked away.

"Darn it! I can't see through these tears," she said. Mindy raised her head to the sky.

Boone reached over and wiped her eyes. "Go ahead. You can do it. You're doing good." He turned his attention to Lucas. "Okay, brother, hang on." Boone felt stupid and worthless. All he could do was encourage Lucas and Mindy and act like a human anchor. He cursed.

Mindy dug for four or five agonizing minutes, first tenderly, then with more effort. Finally, she pulled out a round metal pellet. She handed it to Boone, and then sat back.

"Do you want me to take over now?" Boone prayed the small woman would say no—she'd already proven that she was braver than he was.

"No. Just give me a minute." When she was ready, she dug out a needle, threaded it with the boiled horsehair and began to stitch the wound. Afterwards, she poured the rest of the water from Boone's hat over the site.

"Done . . . already?" Lucas asked. His eyes were cloudy and glazed with pain.

Mindy shrugged herself to her feet and stumbled a few feet away. She began to retch. Then she crumpled at the water's edge, splashing water on her face and crying. As Boone watched, she folded her hands and raised her voice. "Lord, I believe this is a good man. In spite of what I've done, I'd ask you to look over him. Please don't let him die."

Boone eased off Lucas and looked up into the sky. He wasn't a praying man either, but he added a sincere "Amen" to her prayer. He was surprised to find his eyes were wet, and he blinked the moisture away, shaking his head.

*

"You did good," he told Mindy a little later as they sat before the fire watching the flames lick the pieces of wood.

"At least he's passed out now. He can get some rest."

"I mean it," Boone said. He looked her over. Mindy's hair still hung in ratty waves around her shoulders, and though she looked like she had aged ten years, she looked like heaven to him. "You did good."

"Oh, Boone. I've never dealt with anything like that! What if he dies?" Mindy's eyes grew wide and started to well. Boone instinctively scooted closer. He wrapped an arm around her shoulder, and was caught off guard when she flung herself into his arms. He rocked backwards from the blow, but held her, feeling her sweet softness, and cursing himself for thinking of it at a time like this. "Shhhh. You did good. You did good."

Boone rocked her back and forth while she cried. In a little while, her breathing became even. He glanced down to see that she slept. He'd never had a woman cry herself to sleep in his arms before and it was a strange feeling, but then he was feeling all sorts of strange things. He knew one thing, he had to get away from this girl—as soon as possible.

Chapter Thirteen

They waited two days before attempting to move Lucas. Mindy washed his wound everyday with water from the stream and it seemed he had passed any risk of infection.

"It's going on three days now," Mindy chirped as she worked over Lucas. "I think God decided to take a hand in the matter." She smiled at Boone, who grimaced.

Mindy guarded Lucas like a mother hen, clucking over his every desire and need. As far as Boone was concerned, she had seen things no proper female ought to have seen by now. His eyes narrowed at the thought. She waved away his notions of propriety, saying she had nursed her brothers through sickness many times, and the male form was not a novelty to her.

For himself, Lucas doted on the attention, and who wouldn't? He often called to have Mindy fetch him water or to sit by his side and sing.

There Boone grimaced again. Her singing wasn't as lovely as his mother's, that was certain, but it seemed to give Lucas comfort. The sound echoed through the trees and across the water. It made him angry for some reason that he couldn't fathom.

One of the ditties she sang over and over was the song they had listened to at length from the stagecoach driver, Gibb, along their journey. Boone shook his head to think of it. The broken wheel had occurred five days ago, though it seemed like a month.

From his position on the other side of the campfire, Boone watched as Melinda gathered her filthy skirts around her like a lady, and sat down near Lucas. She had ripped off a bit more of her dress to use as a cold compress for his head. She kept it moistened and near in case he called for it. Boone tensed as Mindy laughed.

It was obvious that she was giddy with her success and how well Lucas was progressing.

"Luke! I've sang that song a dozen times. Surely you'd rather hear something else."

Lucas shook his head and held out a hand, which she readily took. "I love to hear you sing. It's so charming hearing Gibb's words coming from your sweet lips."

Mindy blushed. "You're a snake charmer, Luke Wilhite. But you can forget it if you think I'm going to fall for any of that." Still, she was soon singing:

I sing to everybody, in the country and the town,
A song upon a subject that's worthy of renown;
I haven't got a story of fairy-land to broach,
But plead for the cause of sticking to the box seat of a coach.

After singing out the song's final note, Mindy's ringing voice came to a stop. She smiled at Lucas and said, "How was that?"

"Like angels."

Boone snorted and Melinda cast him a wicked frown. "I think I'll go try to trap something for dinner," he said.

Melinda got up and followed him to the tree line. "What's stuck in your craw?" she hissed. "You've been angry as a goat for two days!"

"I don't like to see couples spooning in public!"

"Spooning! I'm trying to give the man a little comfort, is all. He's been shot! He can't move around and he deserves *some* pleasure."

"Well, then, you should stop singing to him!" Boone said.

"Oooh, you make me furious, Boone . . . Boone, what? I don't even know your last name!"

"It's Gary, Gary Boone. *Don't* use it. Boone's fine. As a matter of fact, it's better if you don't call me at all!"

"Oh! You are exactly the type of man my momma warned me about on this trip! You're arrogant and . . . arrogant . . . and I don't know what all, but it's not attractive!"

"Who is there to be attractive for? You?" Boone frowned. "Go look at yourself. You're not a prize! Did your momma ever tell you that?"

Mindy clenched her hands into fists at her sides. "Yes! Yes, as a matter of fact, she did! You'll be happy to know she told me that quite regularly! I realize exactly what I am, *Gary* Boone, and I know what I'm not—which is more than I can say for some people!"

She whirled off, but not before Boone caught a sparkle of moisture in her eyes. He turned and stomped into the forest, slamming his fist against a tree for the second time in a week.

*

Mindy walked down near the water's edge and sat on a rock. She was exhausted, physically and mentally. She caught a glimpse of herself in the murky water and her eyes widened in horror. How could she have thought Lucas had been gently flirting with her? She withdrew into a shell of embarrassment. She looked like something her old cat, Rennie, used to bring up and lay on the back steps. Trembling, she lay her head onto her folded arms and wept.

*

When Boone walked back to the campsite later, he carried two rabbits and a heavy heart. He knew he needed to apologize to Mindy for his behavior earlier, but the words "I'm sorry" didn't come easily. He'd made his mind up, though, and perused the clearing for any sight of her.

Hearing her faint singing, he started off in that direction. As he walked along the water line, he examined his feelings. This girl had him thinking things and acting in ways he'd never thought possible. She'd proven herself over and over on this dusty trail. He could think of settling down with a woman like that. Then he took off his cowboy hat and smacked his leg. What on earth was he thinking along those lines for? She'd made it more than clear she had no feelings for him.

As the singing grew louder, the sound of splashing water began to accompany it. Boone stopped in his tracks. He had an idea of what that meant, especially after he'd chastised her about her appearance. Boone slowly began to move again, his feet acting independently of his brain. Her freshly washed garments were laid out on a boulder to dry in the sun. He swallowed hard.

His head told him what was just around that boulder. His heart urged him on, telling him to claim ignorance when he came upon her. Standing frozen, his heart spoke again, telling him to simply ease up and take a peek. He didn't have to reveal his presence at all. He could make sure she was okay and then return to the campsite.

But her singing told him she was fine. He took a deep breath and prayed for strength. Boone laughed. This little woman was turning him into a praying man, after all.

Turning around and walking back to the clearing where the fire waited was one of the hardest things he'd ever done. But he managed it. He found the rabbits that he'd dropped beside the stones circling the fire and drew out his knife. He took them to the water's edge and began to carve the skin and rip it from the pink meat. He focused his attention on his work and refused to think about what prizes lay just up the creek from him.

Chapter Fourteen

Boone and Mindy eased Lucas into his saddle. Mindy hovered nearby to be sure he wouldn't fall as soon as he was upright. He'd only first sat up the night before, and though he'd done well, and hadn't suffered from any dizziness beyond the first few minutes, she wasn't taking any chances.

"How does that feel?" Boone asked.

"Like a feather bed," Lucas replied. "Let's go. I'm ready to see civilization again." He was hunched over the pommel and white as a newly bleached sheet.

Mindy tut-tutted under her breath and went to climb up on her own horse. It took three hops before she made it into the stirrup and then onto the back of the big animal.

Boone watched from a distance. He had no inclination to help her. Touching her was the farthest thing from his mind—or at least, he tried to put it from his mind. He walked his horse over to her. "You okay?"

She raised her pert nose into the air. "Like you care. What if I said no, Boone? Would you jump to help?"

"I'm trying to be nice, here," he spat. "You've been amazing; you did an amazing thing. I don't want to take anything away from that."

Mindy stiffened her shoulders. "You'll never take anything from me, Gary Boone. I'll see to that."

"Will you shut up and listen for a minute? I'm trying to apologize and you're making it awfully difficult!"

"Well, pardon me! I guess most girls turn and bat their eyes when you turn all syrupy, but I'm not most girls."

"Syrupy! Because I'm trying to say I'm sorry?" Boone's insides clenched. This is why a man didn't apologize for his actions! He glared at her.

Mindy glared back.

From behind, Lucas said, "I don't mean to interrupt, but I'd appreciate if we could get going."

"See what you've done?" Mindy said, kicking her horse forward.

*

They only managed about six miles that day, and even that seemed more than Lucas could bear. By the time they stopped, Mindy noticed a small amount of blood on his freshly washed shirt. She instantly sprang into action, ordering the big man to lie down and let her check the site of the wound.

Her hands were quickly unbuttoning his silk shirt and in a moment, one sweet hand was feeling the spot of the gunshot. Boone watched in shock while Lucas smiled.

"There's too much heat here to suit me," she said. "We're going to have to take it slower." She looked at Boone. "Or should we go faster?"

Boone shrugged. At this minute, Lucas could have died on the spot and he wouldn't have spent a moment in disappointment. "How should I know? You're the doctor."

While Mindy doted on the blond-headed man, Boone stomped into the woods and collected what he needed for a fire. Soon a roaring blaze was going.

"It'll be twilight before long," Boone said. "I'm going to see what I can find for supper." He was confused about his feelings. He liked Lucas, but had begun to think of him as a rival for Melinda's affections. He was so frustrated he didn't know whether to scratch his tail or wind his watch. "I'll be back."

Mindy, distracted, just nodded.

*

Boone was busy creating a simple springle by twisting a flexible piece of green wood into a hoop and sticking both ends in the ground. He tied a short piece of string to one end and then baited it with berries he found nearby. He stretched out a little distance away to await an unsuspecting hare or squirrel.

Just as he closed his eyes for a doze, he was startled by the presence of two men standing over him.

One held a wicked knife and the other a gun. The Byler brothers, Lee and Rich, smiled at one another and then at their captive. "Looks like we meet again, cowboy," Lee said. "I feel right sure our paths are determined to cross until I get what I'm after. From what that girl said, you know more about the gold than you've let on."

"That girl is crazy," Boone replied.

"Maybe so, but me and my little brother here are aiming to find out exactly what she was trying to say." Lee gestured to Rich. "Take his vest."

Boone considered struggling as Rich wrenched the piece of clothing from him, but decided against it. Let 'em have the money—he wanted to be sure to get back to Mindy and Lucas, if possible.

"Hoo-wee, Lee!" Rich said after ripping open the lining of Boone's vest. "Here it is! Cash and bonds, though. No gold." He counted quickly, stumbling several times, before he said, "There's more than three thousand dollars here, brother!"

Lee grinned and took the stack of papers. "This is my money you were hiding, friend, and I don't take too kindly to having to search for it." He gestured to Rich again. "Take care of him. And I don't want to see any gut-shots. Make it permanent." He turned to walk away.

Rich glanced at his brother in surprise. "Me? Why me?"

"You're the one with the gun, stupid. Make it quick, we don't know where that other fellow is." He stomped through the bushes counting the cash.

Rich looked down at Boone and shrugged. He aimed the weapon carefully.

Boone's mouth was dry. He had known that his job was a dangerous one, but it never occurred to him that it might end this way. He immediately thought of Mindy, but then tried to dispel her from his mind. Lucas would take care of her. His mom was his last thought as the gun fired.

*

At the campsite, Mindy was warming beef jerky and water in her tin cup to make a simple broth for Lucas. When she heard the shot, she instinctively looked toward her bag. It sat closed and untouched and she knew her gun was inside. As a matter of fact, she had been chastised repeatedly to keep it out and nearby whenever Boone was gone.

Jumping up, she began running through the woods. Branches and briars pulled at her dress and her flesh, but she was unmindful. "Boone!" she cried. "Boone, where are you?"

After a few yards, she picked up a faint trail made by deer and followed it, hoping Boone would have done the same. She continued to holler his name as she ran. Finally, she stopped. The trail had played out. "Boone!" She glanced around her, and spied the rabbit trap. She knew he was close by.

Mindy began making an ever-widening circle. "Boone! You idiot, don't scare me like this! Where are you?" Panic had begun to set in.

Creeping through the brambles and branches, Mindy almost stumbled over him. His lifeless body was laying partially hidden in a close copse of trees. She fell to his side. There was a wound to the left side of his head. He had been struck by a bullet—the wound was deep but she hoped not life-threatening. Blood still poured from it, a good sign.

Mindy's vision was clouded by tears. "Boone! Wake up! Wake up." She crumpled onto his chest. "Wake up," she cried. "You big oaf, quit scaring me! You can't die!"

Boone moaned. Mindy sat back up and took great gulps of air, hiccupping. "Boone. Can you hear me? Look at me!"

Though slight in form, she suddenly had added strength. She grabbed Boone by his shirt collars and shook him. "Wake up!"

Chapter Fifteen

Boone grunted.

Mindy fell on his chest crying with relief. "Can you hear me?" she asked. "I need you! You have to be all right."

"I'm not . . . too good, actually." Boone struggled to sit up. Melinda grabbed his arms and pulled him upright.

"What happened?"

"The Byler brothers came by . . . for another visit." He glanced around dazedly, seeking his discarded vest. Picking it up, he checked the linings. "They took the money."

"To the dickens with the money, Gary Boone!" She snatched the vest away and pressed it to his wound. "You're bleeding like a stuck pig. We've got to get you back to camp."

"I *would* be a dead man if that Byler fellow had been shooting with his good hand. I don't guess he's as good an aim with his left. He had the right one bandaged."

"It's bad enough as it is! Can you walk?"

Boone struggled to stand. Mindy grasped him around the waist and he leaned his weight against her. She bent down and grabbed his hat.

"Did we catch a rabbit yet?" Boone's lips went up in a smirk.

Mindy started crying all over again. "I don't know, you idiot. I don't care about food right now!"

"Really? What is it you care about? I sure didn't think you'd care if I was shot dead."

"Of course I'd care! What do you think I am? I need you!"

Boone's eyebrows lifted.

"That is, I need you to help me care for Lucas."

"Oh. Of course."

"What did you think I meant? Just for hunting food?"

"No. Never mind."

They arrived at the campsite to see Lucas sitting upright against a fallen log. He was poking the fire and adding twigs. When he saw them coming, he attempted to stand.

"No, no." Boone waved a hand and then gestured to Mindy. "I'm okay. I've got the doctor here."

"What happened?" Lucas asked. "I woke up when I heard a gunshot. I assumed it was you hunting for supper, but I take it our friends have been back?"

"Yeah, but they didn't know you've been shot. They weren't interested in coming here. They just wanted the money." He limped to the log and sat down, weaving slightly.

"What money?" Lucas asked with a guarded look.

"Oh, this cunning thief here has had the money all along!" Mindy said.

"What? You're the reason everyone's getting killed?"

Boone cursed. "No, of course not. Those men planned to rob the stage. We would have all been killed."

Mindy stood with her hands on her hips. "Well, what am I supposed to do now? I've got two cripples on my hands!"

"I'm not a cripple!" both men said together.

"Wait just a cotton-picking minute, little lady," Boone said. "Have I asked anything of you? No, I haven't, and I don't plan to!"

"I didn't mean it like that. Of course, I'll take care of you . . . both, but at this rate, we'll all be dead before we arrive in Tipton!"

"You take care of Lucas! I'll see to myself," Boone growled. He staggered to his feet and lurched to the edge of the stream. He dug his hands into the water and splashed the cooling liquid against his face and head.

"Don't be ridiculous," Mindy said, walking over to him. "Here, let me see it."

"Get away from me! Go tend to Lucas!"

"What's wrong with you? I'm only trying to see how bad the wound is!"

"It's fine. Just a graze." He pulled a bandana out of his back pocket, drenched it in the creek, and then tied it around his head. "See? All better. Go back to your other patient."

Mindy whirled away and stomped back to the fire site. "Patience . . . and faith," she mumbled. "Lord, please give me patience and faith! Men!"

Back at the waterside, Boone was holding his wounded head. "Women!"

*

Mindy went to check on the horses and came back looking dejected. "Well, we're on foot again."

"They took the horses?" Boone guessed.

"Yes. How are we ever going to make it?" Mindy slumped to the ground. "I've had it. I've had it with this trip, with you men, and with dodging bullets every other minute. Please, someone tell me this has all been a bad dream." She gazed over at the men's solemn faces. "I'm sorry." Mindy lowered her head into her hands.

Boone walked over to her and stood awkwardly. He didn't know whether to sit down or continue standing. She looked up at him. "It'll be okay," he said. "We're still alive. It's not that much farther to town." He wanted to be tender and kind, but knew by now that Mindy would respond better to a challenge. "You don't need to start your caterwauling now!"

"I'm not caterwauling! I'm fine," Mindy said. She raised her head and looked deep into Boone's eyes. "Why didn't you just give them the money before?"

Boone didn't answer. He cursed and walked away.

*

The next morning, they set out as soon as the sun peeked over the horizon. Lucas struggled but remained upright, moving slowly. They had traveled approximately a mile when they heard a shout: "Hello! Is anybody out there?"

The trio exchanged glances. The immediate desire was to call out in response, but prudence stopped them.

"Hello?" The call came again, closer this time, and from above. "If you can hear me, holler out! It's okay! I'm with the stage line! Hello!"

Mindy's shoulders dropped in relief. Boone and Lucas smiled. "Here! We're down here!" Lucas called back. "Down by the water!"

"Hold on," said the voice. "I'm coming down!"

In a moment, a horse and rider came through an expanse of trees. He stopped short upon seeing the three. "What the heck happened? Where are the rest of the passengers? Where's Gibb?"

"Dead. They're all dead."

"Dead!" The man was a wiry thing. He looked ancient, with gray hair and kind eyes. "Was it thieves?"

"Yep. They got the money," Boone said. "I'm Marshal Gary Boone. I was along for the ride and supposed to be guarding it. You could say we ran into more than we bargained for."

Mindy's eyes had widened with the knowledge that Boone was a member of law forces. "You're a marshal? Why didn't you tell us?"

"Drop it, Mindy. I had a job to do. All that matters is I failed."

Chapter Sixteen

There was one more night to get through in the journey toward their destination. The scrawny old man had promised to send help by the morrow. Mindy had been given the option to ride along, but wouldn't leave her charges.

Lucas and Boone began to grow antsy and ill-tempered as they realized they would soon be home. They were ready to be on with their lives.

As dusk turned into a deepening twilight, the three sat fireside, studying one another, lost in thought. A chilly wind had swept in and they were huddled close to the warmth of the flickering flames.

"So, you never told us what you were doing on this trip in the first place," Boone said, looking at Mindy. "Why would a young lady be traveling alone?"

Mindy sniffed. "It was supposed to be a simple trip from Mississippi to Kansas to pick up a title to property left us by my uncle. Have you heard of The Blue Saloon? That's where it's being held."

"A saloon? Well, that's a great way to end a trip like this!" Boone said, with fire in his eyes.

"I only plan to pick up the title, not apply for employment."

"Has anyone ever told you that you can be a little stupid? A nice lady doesn't travel alone in these parts. She certainly wouldn't visit establishments like that, either. Have you thought about what would have happened to you if you had ridden along with Gibb? Have you considered that at all?"

"Yes," Mindy said. "I thought about that as soon as I saw him. I could have been lying there alongside him."

"Only if you were lucky! Those men would have carted you off with them . . . for more than an afternoon ride into the country."

Mindy blanched. That thought had not occurred to her.

"What if Lucas, here, or—me—weren't gentlemen?"

She snorted. "Perhaps I *would* have been better off with the Bylers, if *you* represent a gentleman."

Boone stared hard into her green eyes. "I'm being serious. You have to be more careful. What if we leave you in Tipton and you go off on another harebrained adventure?"

"I don't plan to go off on another adventure, Gary Boone! I didn't plan on this one! And besides, when I get to Tipton, I'll be no concern of yours, anyway. What do you care?"

Rubbing his hands and holding them in front of the fire, Lucas joined in. "You two never stop, do you? Can you leave go for a while, at least?"

"Stupid," Boone said. "You can't fix stupid. My momma always said you can love it and you can pet it, but you can't fix it."

Mindy's body drew up into a hard line. "How dare you say something like that! You don't know me! You don't know anything about me!"

It was Boone's turn to snort. "I reckon I do. We've spent every minute together for the last . . . six days. I've seen what I need to see to sum you up pretty well."

"Well, that makes two of us! And do you want to know what I've decided? You're a heathen! A filthy, good-for-nothing heathen! You can't see anything past the end of your nose!" Mindy stood up and walked off into the woods.

The two men stared at each other. "Do you think she's gone off to take care of business, or decided to walk on to Tipton without us?" Lucas finally said.

Boone cursed and stood up. He stalked to the edge of the forest line. "Mindy! Mindy?" He glanced back at Lucas, then straightened his shoulders and strode into the brambles.

Boone heard the sound of sobbing and it wrenched his gut. How many times had she cried in the last few days? Enough to wash away every sin he'd ever had, that was for sure. Too bad it wouldn't work. He crept up to her softly. "Mindy, are you okay?"

"Yes! Of course I'm okay! I'm always okay! That's my lot in life. When my brothers got hurt and had to be stitched up, it was my job to do it. When my friends got married and asked me to stand beside them, it was my job to do that, too. When my dad died and my mom fell apart, who took care of *her*—even though I was falling apart inside? Me! And I was fine. I have to be fine. There's no other choice."

Boone stepped up to her, backing her against a tree. "You don't have to carry the weight of the world, Mindy. You could ask for help."

"From who, my little brothers? You?"

"Maybe." He leaned in and looked into her eyes. The night enveloped them, creating a quiet place where nothing moved. He raised a calloused hand to her cheek. "So pretty."

"Pretty?" Mindy said, with a voice that trembled. "Not me. Never."

"Yep. Even with the mud and the mess, you're one of the prettiest things I ever saw." Boone smiled, and Mindy stared into his black eyes.

Boone leaned in closer . . . closer. Softly, his lips touched hers, surprised when her lips turned up to tentatively meet his. He stepped closer, placing one hand on her slender waist. As she leaned into the kiss, he pulled her even closer, deepening the experience for both of them.

Mindy made a small sound at the back of her throat, and Boone's head started to burn. He placed his arms around her and pulled her against him, changing the small, innocent kiss into something more. He swam in the moment. Plunging headfirst into waters that he knew were dangerous. His heart stepped in, crinkling in an odd sort of way as it dashed itself against the rocky borders of possibility.

Reluctantly, Boone pulled back. He leaned his forehead against hers, breathing deeply.

*

Mindy gasped. "What was that?" she said softly with a faint smile. Her breath whispered past his face.

"That was a kiss, Mindy. You said you'd never had one, remember?"

Suddenly Mindy remembered the rocking stage and her fear that they were all about to plummet over the edge of the cliff. She remembered her panic and the crazy things she had shouted. They came flooding back to her now and she shrank in embarrassment.

"Is that what this was? A pity kiss?" Mindy took a step back as her face drained of color. Quickly she reached and struck Boone across the face.

"What? Pity? Did that *feel* like a pity kiss?" Boone demanded, placing a hand to his blistering cheek.

"I don't know. I'm stupid, remember? How would I know the difference?" She turned from him and marched back toward the fire. Over her shoulder she said, "I'll be sure and ask your wife when we meet."

Chapter Seventeen

Boone slapped his forehead. His wife! Of course! He'd forgotten about the picture of his sister, again. There was no telling what Mindy thought of him, after kissing "another woman."

Figuring she still considered him a shiftless good-for-nothing, Boone shambled back to the clearing where the two others sat. Mindy and Lucas were involved in an animated conversation about their hometowns. Boone was relieved to see that she was no longer sad, but entranced.

"My dad died when I was small," she was saying, "which meant my mom had the burden of raising six children alone—three girls and three boys." She sighed. "You'd love my sisters. They're charming and witty and down-to-earth. They're beautiful and well-mannered . . . nothing at all like me. I was raised with my brothers so I was somewhat of a hoyden, to my mother's dismay." She laughed, a sweet sound that pulled at Boone's heart and head.

"I can't believe you were a trouble to her," Lucas replied.

"Oh, I was! Always getting into trouble and getting dirty. At church services, I'd run off and play with the boys, then come back with my dress in tatters and hanging with filth. Oh, I was a trial!"

"Well, you've grown up now."

Mindy blushed. "Yes, but I've never had my sisters' easy ways. They married respected young men in our community and take part in the social engagements of the town. They make Mother very proud."

"And you haven't got the personality for those things?" Lucas studied Mindy as she formulated her reply.

"It's just that I seem to want different things. I never wanted to settle down with the fellows that came around in the early days. And as the years went on, there were fewer callers. My mother's greatest fear is that I'll end up an old maid like my Aunt Sarah." She laughed again, holding her arms around her knees. "She's probably right. I'd rather travel and see things."

"Doesn't it bother you, not having someone in your life?"

"Sometimes. Mostly, I miss the idea of being a mother. But I can play with my nieces and nephews whenever I want."

Lucas caught her gaze. "It may be that things will change for you on this trip. You may meet someone you can care about." His implication was clear.

Mindy ducked her head. "I don't know. Tomorrow should see me into Tipton, finally, and then I'll be able to pick up that dreadful deed and deal with the property. After that, I'll be headed home again. Hopefully, the return trip won't be so eventful!"

From across the fire, Boone tensed. The idea of Mindy on her way back to Mississippi churned his gut. "You plan to travel alone back to Mississippi?" he interjected.

"Of course," she said. "How else will I get home?"

"I'm not sure, but you can't still think you can handle whatever comes your way! This trip should have made that obvious."

"Maybe she'll find someone to escort her," Lucas said. "There's a possibility I'll be available." He smiled.

"Oh, I couldn't ask you to do that!" Mindy said.

"I do a lot of traveling. Let's just wait to see what the future holds, shall we?"

"That's enough about me," Mindy said. "What are you headed to Tipton for?"

"I've been there several times," Lucas offered. "I've found it to be a wonderful town. It's small, but growing. A man could make a good living there. I've considered buying property and settling down."

"That would be wonderful!"

"Yes," Lucas agreed, "but plans change. I'll wait to see what happens."

Boone grunted and jabbed at the fire. "I think I'll go sleep. Looks like you two would like to be alone."

"What is that supposed to mean?" Mindy asked. "We're just talking."

Boone and Lucas exchanged long looks. Boone made a rude noise. "I'm going to sleep. See y'all in the morning."

*

Mindy glanced to Lucas and shrugged. "Men! Oh, present company excluded, of course."

Lucas smiled and Mindy stared into his blue eyes. He was a tall man and sat ramrod straight. He was attractive in a rough sort of way. Sometimes his eyes were hooded, as if he had seen things he didn't care to remember. He was used to giving orders and being obeyed. Someone had said he'd been an officer in the war and she could believe it. Lucas didn't speak often, but when he did his words were precise and clear, and brooked no argument.

As they continued their conversation, her eyes wandered over to Boone, stretched out near the warmth of the fire. The two men couldn't be more different. Where Lucas was fair, Boone was dark, with black eyes that spoke what he wouldn't say. Her Tormentor was even taller than Lucas, but muscular and swarthy. He had wide shoulders that narrowed into a trim waist, and she frequently found herself watching him walk. He was confident and sure of himself, to the point of cockiness, which often made her mad enough to spit. Just looking at him could make her blood boil. And certainly, his kiss had made her bubble. There was something about Boone that made her think crazy, act crazy. Why, she'd completely forgotten about his wife! He probably thought she was the sort of jezebel her mom sometimes whispered about, returning his kiss like that. She could still feel his lips on hers there in the darkness. Mindy had never imagined a single moment could make you feel so many things at once: dizzy and safe, curious and wise, hungry and—

" . . . are your brothers?" Lucas was asking.

Mindy shook herself. "I'm sorry. I didn't hear what you said."

Lucas followed her eyes to where Boone snoozed. "Never mind. It's getting late. We better get some sleep."

Mindy was startled by the abrupt end to the conversation. "All right." She turned to snuggle into the bed of soft leaves she'd made.

"I enjoyed talking with you, Mindy."

Turning to study Lucas, Mindy replied, "Me too. You're easy to talk with." She blushed again and Lucas smiled. "Good night."

*

When Boone awoke the next morning, there was no sign of Mindy. He glanced over to Lucas, who was adding small twigs to the fire.

Boone leaned against the ground and twisted his body. "I could stretch a mile," he said with a grin, "but I'd have to walk back." His eyes turned serious. "You two have a good, long talk last night?"

Lucas didn't answer immediately. He poked the fire. When he looked up, his eyes were hard. "Is there anything you want to tell me about Mindy?"

"What do you mean? Besides, the fact she's a pain in the backside?"

"No. If you have feelings for her. Sometimes, I get that distinct impression."

"Me? You know we fight like cats and dogs. It's oil and water."

"I'm just letting you know that I care for her. I aim to court her when we get to town and get settled in."

Boone stared into Lucas's eyes and his black eyes grew even darker. "That's fine," he said. "She'll need someone to take care of her and keep her out of trouble."

"I need to know if that's going to be a problem with you."

"Heck no!" Boone stood and dusted off his dungarees. "You're welcome to her and good luck." For some reason the conversation was making him ill. He felt the need to hit something again, but his skin on his hand was still cracked and broken from the last time. He flexed it. "I'm going to wash up."

As he walked to the water's edge, he passed Mindy returning.

She had washed the mud from her face.

"Don't you have more clothes in that bag of yours?" he demanded.

"For your information, there's only one change of clothes in there. As if it's any of your business. I don't see the need to destroy a second dress."

Boone had to admit the logic of that, but was disgruntled by the amount of leg that showed beneath her tattered hem. Fully one half of her white calves was on display. Her brown walking boots did little to cover more than her ankles.

"Perhaps today would be a good day to change, seeing as how we'll be getting into town," he suggested with a grimace, imagining the looks she would receive.

Mindy looked down to her dress and then back at Boone. "Maybe so."

"Do whatever you want," he growled and continued to the stream.

Chapter Eighteen

By midmorning, the trio heard a welcome rumbling as they walked. It turned into a minute dust cloud, which turned into a stagecoach. Salvation had arrived. Mindy's eyes began to tear, and it took all her control not to weep with joy.

Shorty, the wiry old man, was at the reins. He pulled the surefooted steeds to a hard stop, throwing rocks and dirt into the air. "Halloo!" he cried with a wide, snaggle-toothed smile, before leaning over the rail of the coach and spitting a brown stream of tobacco juice onto the hard soil.

"Anybody here ready for a ride?" His smile broadened at the humor of his words.

Mindy leaned against Lucas, gathering strength. "Yes," she said quietly. "Yes. Thank You, Lord."

The two men cheered up noticeably; their backs straightened and their eyes sparkled. "Come on, darlin'," Lucas said, "Let's head for Tipton!" He picked Mindy up and swung her in a wide circle.

"Put me down, you idiot!" Mindy said with glee. "You're going to hurt yourself all over again."

Sure enough, when he set her back on the ground, he gripped his chest with a tender hand, though he winked and said, "It was well worth the pain, my dear!"

Mindy turned and ran to the waiting coach. Boone had slung her bag inside and was holding the door. He wore a grim frown. Mindy ignored him as she climbed into the stagecoach. The faded velvet seating and wood interior made her feel like she had arrived home.

Mindy leaned back in the seat and sighed, as Lucas slapped Boone on the back and climbed aboard. Boone followed, closing the door. Before they were even settled, the driver started the horses into a canter. They were headed back to the land of the living.

*

"So, what'll you do when we get to town?" Mindy asked Boone.

"I don't have much choice. I reckon' I'll be heading out to find that bank money and bring it back."

Mindy shuddered. "You can't mean to chase after those fellows alone?"

"That'll be up to the stage company. I'll be reporting to them when we arrive. But I expect they'll want me to head out as soon as possible. I'll probably visit my mother and then head on out."

"And your wife, I guess."

"Yeah. Of course." Boone mentally smacked himself again. A wife sure was a lot of trouble.

"Oh. By the way, I guess I can give this back to you now," Mindy said reaching into her bag. She extracted a Bible wrapped in cloth and removed a picture from its pages. She handed it over to him. "Funny thing, you had it in your possession the whole time you were carrying my bag." A faint smile crossed her face. "She sure is pretty."

"Yeah," Boone admitted. "She is that."

*

Mindy fell silent. She had thought . . . she wasn't sure what she had thought. But she hadn't expected Boone to be planning to leave even before he arrived in Tipton. She looked out the window, past the faded, oiled-leather curtain. The landscape rolled past at a jarring pace. Again, she felt tears welling up in her eyes, but for the life of her she couldn't be sure why.

*

In less than six hours, Mindy began to see signs that they were nearing civilization again. There was a steady stream of men on horseback traveling along the same road as they drew closer to Tipton. Just outside the town, Mindy saw a long line of wagons that obviously made up a wagon train. In a large, open creek bank, horses and cattle were enjoying the cool water. The sheer number of wagons and livestock was overwhelming. "Now, that's a journey," she commented.

Boone looked out the window on the same side of the coach. "Uh huh. There aren't as many moving west by wagon as there once was. The railroad has cut down on the traffic, but when you're moving your entire household, there isn't much other way."

Mindy watched women working near the wagons. Controlled chaos seemed to reign king. Children galloped and played nearby. "God bless 'em, is all I can say."

Lucas chortled. "Yep."

The stagecoach driver never gave any heed to the increased level of activity on the roads; he still drove like the devil was chasing him. The bouncing and banging reminded Mindy of her earlier complaints. Her attitude had changed, and she relished every jounce. It was better than walking any day.

Mindy watched, fascinated, as they entered into the cluster of buildings making up the town. Lines of wagons were parked along the roadside, forcing the coach to squeeze in between them.

When they pulled to an abrupt halt, Boone was already swinging out the door. Lucas exited and helped Mindy down, and she glanced around, taking in the sights. The wood-frame buildings stretched out in either direction, lining the narrow thoroughfare. Along one side of the street was a two story hotel, Peter's Livery, Feed, and Sale Stable, a barber shop, and a furniture store. Past those, the brick exterior of The Bank of Tipton was visible.

On the other side of the road stood two barrooms side-by-side, next to Kit's Eatery. All along the boardwalks were the good citizens of the town, and the folks securing provisions for the long wagon trip.

Several women cast a wary eye at Melinda as she alighted from the stage; no doubt her red face, mangled hairdo, and inappropriate garb caught their attention. Melinda straightened her shoulders and looked them head on, without shame. She had survived a grand adventure—the likes of which she could tell her nieces and nephews about with great fanfare. Many of the women turned away, not being able to withstand the hard stare Mindy offered.

Lucas arrived at her elbow. "Let me escort you to the hotel and make sure we get you settled in comfortably." He glanced over his shoulder at Boone. "I'll take that bag off your hands now, friend."

Mindy's Tormentor stood still as a statue for a minute, looking at Mindy as if he would speak, but then he merely handed over the piece of luggage. It certainly looked worse for the wear. Mindy hadn't realized until now the beating it had taken.

"Will we see you again before you leave?" Mindy asked.

Boone studied her quietly. "I don't know why. Looks like you've got everything you need."

Mindy glanced up at Lucas who wore a broad smile. "That she does, neighbor, that she does."

The men exchanged glances. "You better do right," Boone said in a hard voice. "I'll be close by, and there's always talk."

"Do right about what?" Mindy asked, glancing from one man to the other.

"I think he gets it."

"I got it. No need for worries. See to your own troubles. Let us know if you make it back all right." Lucas was being extremely magnanimous.

Looking at Boone, Mindy realized that this moment might be the last she would see him. Without considering her actions, she threw her arms around his neck, surprising them both. "Thanks for all you've done." She leaned against him and said in a quieter voice. "I take back what I said—your wife *is* a lucky woman."

Boone took her by the arms and set her away from him. "I better go." He tipped his hat once and turned on his heel. Mindy watched him walk away.

Chapter Nineteen

"Come on," Lucas said, moving with a light step. "Let's get you checked into the hotel." He tugged at Mindy's arm.

Turning, Mindy sighed. It seemed her heart had dropped into her stomach.

"I've stayed here several times, and I feel sure you'll like it." Lucas's grin made him seem sweet and appealing. "Hot meals are provided each day, and the owners offer tokens for the plunge bath down the road."

The idea of a bath caught Mindy's attention. "Oh, that would be heavenly!"

"Shorty said they were sending a stage to pick up our luggage. It should be here by tomorrow or the next day. If you have need of anything in the meantime, I hope you'll let me know."

"That's all right. I have my own money. And besides, I would never take yours."

"I hope the day will come when you may accept more than that from me, Mindy." They had reached the wooden boardwalk and he turned her to face him. "I'd like the opportunity to call on you."

"What?" Mindy said.

"Surely you've realized by now that I have feelings for you, Mindy. I know this isn't the appropriate time or place. I had planned to discuss it over dinner tonight, but, well . . . " He shrugged and smiled.

Mindy was startled . . . and flattered, but beyond that, she wasn't sure what she felt.

"You don't have to answer me now. Think about it, and we'll discuss it more over our meal." He took her arm and wrapped it over his, patting it gently. "Don't worry. Everything will work out." With that, he escorted her into the sumptuous hostel.

*

It took a moment for Mindy's eyes to adjust after the bright sunlight. Once they did, she gasped. The interior of the hotel was sumptuously appointed, with floor to ceiling columns and rich, maple furniture. A piano sat to one side of the large receiving area and a writing desk sat to another. The walls were painted stark white and decorated with elaborate wooden trim painted the same shade. Cozy armchairs were scattered here and there. The reception desk sat at the far wall, and four large, crystal chandeliers hung from the ceiling.

Mindy moved slowly through the room, touching various pieces of furniture and studying the patterned Brussels carpet beneath her feet.

"Is it okay to walk on this?" Mindy leaned over conspiratorially. "My shoes are filthy!"

"This hotel caters to ranchers and cowboys, among others. They're used to much worse than dirt on these floors!" Lucas laughed.

A man approached wearing a sharp uniform and addressed Lucas. "It's good to see you again, Mr. Wilhite. Will you be staying?" Mindy was surprised that he seemed to pay no attention to her state of dress or disheveled appearance.

"Yes, Curtis. I'll need a room for myself and a room for Miss McCorkle. Please give her your best."

"Nothing less." The man named Curtis looked around them. "Are you carrying luggage, sir?"

"It hasn't arrived, but we expect it tomorrow or the next day. Our driver said they've sent another stage after it. Please send Miss McCorkle's to her room as soon as it arrives." Lucas glanced at the dining room entrance. "Are the supper seatings still at five and seven o'clock?"

"They are, Mr. Wilhite. When would you like to dine?" Lucas told the man to save a table for them at the late meal.

Mindy listened to the conversation, faintly irritated that she had not been consulted. As good as food sounded, a bath and a good night's sleep in a comfortable bed sounded even more appealing.

"Curtis, Miss McCorkle will want to visit the baths. Could we have our tokens immediately?"

"Of course, sir." Curtis spun and headed to the reception desk to take care of the request.

When the man left, Mindy looked at Lucas. Her mouth was set in a hard line. "Lucas!" she hissed. "I can't afford the most expensive room in the hotel!"

"Don't worry about the details, Mindy. Leave them to me."

Curtis returned with two keys. "May I escort you?"

"Not necessary. I'll see Miss McCorkle to her room. Thank you."

Together they walked through the lobby to a carpeted staircase. Lucas knew the way and soon had Mindy at her door. "I'll leave you here. I look forward to seeing you at dinner."

They said their goodbyes and Mindy stepped into her room. She was instantly taken aback by the decor and lavishness. She had a corner room on the second floor. White curtains fluttered in two windows.

A large, mahogany bed sat catty-cornered to the room, and a writing desk, chairs and fireplace completed the picture. Mindy sighed, wanting more than anything to fall into bed and sleep for hours. But she knew she'd feel better when she was clean again.

*

The bathhouse was a long structure with high ceilings and a large pool for bathing. It was intended for multiple guests at once. Thankfully, Mindy was able to secure a private room for her ablutions. She sank into the galvanized tub full of hot water and drifted away. When she awoke, the water was cool and she had to hurry to get ready for the evening.

The extra dress she had packed was a simple frock, but it was clean. Mindy delighted in sliding into the garment. She pulled her hair back and tied it with a ribbon, and felt like she could pass for a respectable female again.

Walking back to the hotel, she scanned the buildings around her for sight of The Blue Saloon, with no luck. *Another day.*

She arrived a bit after seven and went straight to the dining area where Lucas awaited. His eyes grew wide when she entered. "How lovely you look!"

Chapter Twenty

June 14, 1880

Dear Mother,

I am finally situated in Tipton and able to catch you up on what has happened since my last letter. I have only just arrived after another uneventful stage in my journey. Traveling can be _so_ monotonous!

I am currently domiciled in the Golden Hotel and, believe it or not, I am staying in the brides' room! It is a feast for the eyes, and I know you would enjoy seeing the fancy embellishments. (Do not worry, there is nothing new to report—I have only reserved the room for one.)

You might be surprised to learn I have met a man who seems smitten with me. The very idea makes my head swell to unreasonable proportions. I cannot remember the last time I was even regarded by a man! And Mother, he has asked if he may call on me.

Tonight we dined together in the hotel's supper room. It was a delight. The food was cooked to perfection—I had the roast with potatoes and gravy and cathead biscuits, and it was as good as your own. We know what a high standard that is! Over our meal, as the gas lamps burned above us in a romantic sort of way, he asked if I might be willing to allow him to court me publicly. I believe I appeared to be calm, but inside I was shaking like the proverbial leaf! I never thought the day would come. Can it be that I might have children in my future? I dare not begin to even think of such things at this point.

I will spend a moment describing him to you. By my best estimate, he is in his late forties and was involved in some war or another. He is a proud man, straight in his bearing, and you can well see the result of many years of army life. He is used to giving orders and being obeyed without question. (This might cause a bit of a problem between us, for you know how stubborn I can be at times.) He is very tall, blond of hair, and blue of eye. He is kind, treats me well, and is generous to a fault. You would like him, I think.

I've met another man as well. He is a great, uncouth brute with no regard for polite society. He is dark where Lucas is fair, wide where Lucas is slim. I don't know why I even mention him except that we spent a great deal of time in each other's company on the stage ride here. He is a marshal and has a terribly dangerous job. I had no idea how violent the area could be . . . of course, I only go by what I am told.

I am well, and glad to be at my destination. I will seek out the location of the tavern on the morrow and will write again as I prepare to leave to let you know to watch for me. I have hopes that I can retrieve the deed and, perhaps with the bank's help, find someone interested in purchasing the property. High hopes, indeed!

Speaking of hopes, I am hoping that this letter finds you well and that the boys are not giving you fits. Please say hello to the sisters and give each of my nieces and nephews kisses. I miss you all so much!

By the by, I have noticed that the ladies here are wearing a lovely poplin-type of fabric. I will strive to bring some home, along with gifts for the little ones.

Mother, I had no idea how much I would miss your smile and companionship. Please take care of yourself until my return. Until then,

I remain your loving daughter,
Melinda

*

Boone strode into the family home in a bad temper. His mother was shelling peas and guessed his irritable mood as she rose from the table to greet him.

She gently touched the spot where the bandana covered his head, kissed his cheek, and said, "I take it things did not go as planned."

"No! And I'm mad enough to swallow a horned-toad backwards. We were ambushed by thieves who took the money from the stage."

"What will you do now?"

"I'm waiting to hear from the stage line, but I plan to go after the men who did it and get that money back. I had a job to do, and it rankles that I didn't get to see it through!"

"Well, not meaning to change the subject, but do you care to tell me what happened to your head?"

"I'd rather not say."

Mrs. Boone dropped into a chair. "Gary Boone, what am I going to do with you? One day they're going to send you home in a box!"

"It's just a graze, Mother."

"That may be so, but let's unwrap you and take a look." She ushered Boone into the kitchen and sat him down in a ladder-back chair. He winced when the cloth was pulled away. "Tsk, tsk, tsk," she clucked. "It's a mite more than a graze. God was watching over you this time, son. I'm afraid all I can do is clean it and wrap it again. You're going to have a dreadful scar."

Boone smiled. "Don't worry about that. It'll give me more respectability among the other men."

"If looking like a dime's worth of dog meat is what you're aiming for, you've succeeded. Let me get the antiseptic."

As she dabbed at the wound, Boone cleared his throat. "Tell me again about you and my father."

"Oh, that's an old story. One you've heard countless times. You don't want to hear it again." Mrs. Boone paused in her ministrations. She gripped her son's chin and looked him in the eyes. "What's got into you, asking about a thing like that?"

"How did you feel when he left? I don't remember any of it."

"I was brokenhearted. Still am. He was the only man I ever loved." She grinned. "Except for you, of course."

"What happened?"

"Oh . . . Your father wanted different things. He wanted to follow the gold rush and live day-to-day. He was happiest when he was up to his neck in trouble. Sometimes I think you take after him in that way. After you were born, I had the urge to settle down permanent. We couldn't make each other happy, I guess."

Boone looked thoughtfully off into space.

"Gary Boone. I can see those wheels turning. What's on your mind? Is it a girl?"

"Yeah, I reckon it is. But she's not available and she doesn't think I am, either." He glanced up at his mother. "I think you'd like her. She reminds me a little of you."

"Well, she must be a fine girl, indeed!"

"Are you about done there?" The antiseptic burned and Boone had other things on his mind. He wanted to clean up and eat. He felt like he could sleep forever and a day, and he couldn't wait for nightfall.

"Yes. And I suppose you're starving. Let me check the larder and see what I have." She bustled off and was soon singing a song while she worked.

Boone watched her in the kitchen for a few minutes, and then shook himself. He had things to do.

Chapter Twenty-One

To her surprise, Melinda rose with the sun. After a night in a real bed, she felt refreshed and energized. She had a lot of things to accomplish, and was anxious to get started. Once she dressed, she sat at the little writing desk to make a list:

Blue Tavern — deed, Mr. William Kirby

Undertaker—settle account

General store—items for mother and children

Post letter

Hotel—arrange for a smaller room

When she finished, she held the paper up, deciding to speak to the undertaker first. Her uncle had passed away three months before, and though she hadn't known him at all, she felt saddened that he was laid to rest without family nearby. She added "Visit grave" to her list.

She gathered her reticule and exited the hotel, asking for directions to the undertaker's salon as she passed through the lobby.

*

Boone stopped in at the general store to see if there was any word from his superiors at the stage line. The telegraph operator—who happened to be the owner's son—reported that there had been no messages all morning.

"The only communication we've had in days is this letter for a lady who's supposed to arrive in town soon." As he waved it, Boone caught the name: Miss Mindy McCorkle. His eyebrows rose, but he said nothing.

Instead, he put sixty-five cents on the counter for a can of oysters and, after thinking about it, added another quarter for crackers. There was a group of men gathered in the back of the store discussing politics, and he meandered over to listen while he ate his snack.

In a few minutes, an attractive young lady came in the door; by her side was a little blond-headed imp.

"Uncle Gary!" the child squealed, running for Boone's arms. He picked her up and tossed her high, earning delighted cries.

"How's my best girl?"

"Good." She paused and fluttered her little lashes. "Uncle Gary? Mommy said I can't have candy until after lunch."

"What!" Boone replied in mock horror. "The very idea."

The little girl nodded.

"We'll see about that! Since I'm buying lunch today, I get to decide what's on the menu, and it so happens the first thing is a piece of peppermint candy." His eyes sparkled.

"Hurray!"

"Why do you do these things, Gary?" Boone's sister asked. "You know Terese doesn't mind me at all when you're about." She sighed.

"That's okay. She has to mind all day long, every day. Sometimes it's fun to break the rules. Isn't it, Terri?"

"Terese, please," Boone's sister said.

"Uncle Gary? What happened to your head?"

Boone put on a fierce face. "I was fighting a bear and he got me!"

The girl giggled. "Was it a big bear?"

"The biggest bear you ever saw!" He squeezed his niece tight. "He was a talking bear! He said he was hunting little girls who eat candy before lunch!" He goosed her in the tummy and she squealed again.

"Gary, please. You're causing people to stare."

Boone looked up and saw Mindy McCorkle was watching him, having arrived in the store while he played. This was a radiant version of the Mindy he was used to and he stared for perhaps a moment too long.

Mindy regarded the trio from a distance, her green eyes speaking volumes, before she stepped up to the counter to see about posting a letter. There she was informed there was a missive waiting for her as well. She tucked the envelope into her bag.

Finished, she began perusing the fabrics piled high on a long table. Boone walked over to her with Terese in his arms, leaving his sister, Becky, studying items on a shelf. "Aren't you going to say hello?"

"You looked busy," she said indicating the lady behind him. "She's very pretty. You're a lucky man." Mindy glanced at the girl in his arms. "She looks very much like you." Then she held out her hand. "Hello! My name is Mindy, what's yours?"

"Terri," the little girl replied, laying her cheek against Boone's shoulder.

"Don't tell me you *like* this great big brute who's holding you!" Mindy teased.

Blond hair bobbed as the girl nodded her head vigorously.

Boone studied the woman before him as she carried on the one-sided conversation. Her face was blistered and peeling, and she had lost a few pounds, but she looked wonderful. She seemed to be very comfortable talking to the small child in his arms. She was a natural at it, although Terese was showing her shy side.

"You look like a big girl." Mindy touched a blond ringlet. "I imagine you're a big help to your mother, aren't you?"

"She can be," said a voice as Becky joined them. "She can also be a hooligan." Becky gazed at her daughter with a proud smile.

"She's adorable," Mindy said.

"Yes, she is. But she knows it. She uses it to her advantage whenever possible." Both women smiled.

"I remember a young girl who did the same at her age." Mindy's eyes glowed.

"I'm Becky," said the one, holding out her hand. "I'm pleased to meet you."

Mindy grasped it and introduced herself. "Boone and I traveled together on the stage."

"Oh my! I hope you're all right! It sounds like it was a terrible ordeal!"

"It wasn't as bad as all that. Now that I've had a good meal and some rest, it seems more and more like a very bad dream." Mindy gave Boone a pointed stare and he frowned.

"I see you're looking at the calicos. Mr. Green has a lovely selection."

"Yes, I promised my mother I'd look in on the yard goods. This is a beautiful color."

Becky leaned in conspiratorially. "Yes, but it's a bit high. He gets ten cents a yard."

Mindy's eyes widened.

"I can see where this conversation is headed," Boone said, rolling his dark eyes. "If you'll both excuse us, Terri and I are off to the candy jar."

*

"He's a good man, I think," Mindy said, watching Boone walk away. "He can be gruff, but I'm learning it's just his way."

"Yes, he *is* a good man," Becky said, looking from Mindy to Boone and back again. "One of the best."

"He thinks you're special, too. You should know he treasures your photo."

"Really?" Becky eyes widened. "That surprises me."

"It shouldn't. I hope every husband would feel the same."

Becky paused. "Yesss . . . I suppose they would. Are you referring . . . ?"

"He helped keep us alive on the trip. I don't know if he would brag on himself, but he was very brave," Mindy admitted the information to her chagrin.

"Yes. I suppose so." Becky glanced over to where Boone and Terese were licking peppermint sticks. "Did . . . my *husband* . . . say anything else?"

Mindy blushed brightly. "No, not really. There wasn't much

time for that kind of talk."

"I see. Well, it was very nice talking with you. I hope to see you again."

"Yes," Mindy said faintly. "Perhaps."

Becky turned to join her husband and child and Mindy watched as the lovely lady began whispering to Boone. He listened for a moment and then glanced up to meet Mindy's gaze.

Suddenly, Mindy felt like she might be sick. She could look at the fabrics another time. Whirling, she left the store. Outside, she stood trying to decide where to go. Her legs felt rubbery.

"Where are you headed in such a hurry?" A deep voice came from behind her. "You look a little lost." It was Boone. Tall, dark, handsome Boone.

Mindy took a deep breath and exhaled. "I'm wondering which direction I should go," she said too quickly. "I'm not sure where The Blue Tavern is . . . and I was going to ask for directions from the shop keeper, but then . . . I . . . I . . . " She stared up into black eyes. "I decided to come outside for some air."

"You can't go to the saloon by yourself!"

Mindy bristled. What was wrong with her? This man drove her insane! "I suppose I can!"

"Where's Lucas?" Boone growled. "Why isn't he with you? You can't just waltz into a bar unaccompanied!"

"It's the middle of the day, for heaven's sake! I'm just going to meet with the owner for a few minutes."

Boone stared up the street and his jaw clenched. He removed his hat and rubbed his head vigorously. "Well, I sure won't let you go alone. I'm coming with you!"

Mindy gestured to the store. "What about . . . ?"

"Never mind! Let's go!"

Chapter Twenty-Two

Boone strode along the plank boardwalk toward the saloon and Mindy had to scurry to catch up.

"What on earth is the matter with you?" she said. "Why are you in such a hurry?"

"I want to get this taken care of. Get that deed in your hand, so I won't have to worry about you anymore."

"You're worrying about me?"

He glanced her way. Her hair was tied into a severe knot on the back of her head, and for a moment he regretted that it wasn't hanging down in a ratty, passionate mess like before.

"I'd worry about any woman who does a foolish thing like this." He never slowed his pace.

"It's not 'foolish,' I'll thank you to know. That deed is the entire reason I'm on this trip!"

They passed several establishments: a drug store with a doctor's office above it that had a small sign reading *Lending Library* and pointing up the stairs, a newspaper office, and a blacksmith shop, where the smithy was busy pounding against a flaming horseshoe. Mindy's head turned back and forth as she tried to take in the sights around her.

"This is a big place. I had no idea Tipton was so . . . advanced," she said.

"Why? 'Cause it's stuck in the middle of nowhere? There's a lot more going on than you can see. You can't always judge things on first appearances."

"Why do you have to take such a tone with me? I didn't say anything wrong," Mindy stormed.

Boone stopped abruptly, and she ran into him. He grabbed her by the shoulders and set her back a step, then stared into her eyes. "Because you make me crazy. I don't know what it is about you, but you make my insides twist up."

"Me?"

"Yes, you." Boone's voice was husky. Just then he took Mindy by the hand and dragged her across the street. Above one of the buildings was a shabby sign with a name painted on it: *The Blue Saloon*. They reached the plank door and Boone demanded, "Wait here."

"I will not!" Mindy said, stomping one dainty foot.

"Oh, yes you will. You'll wait right here by this door, and you won't move a muscle, or I'll . . . "

"What? What will you do? I'd really like to know. And I'm sure all these fine people would like to know as well!" Mindy gestured down the boardwalk where women in long day dresses stared openly.

Boone realized they were becoming an object of attention. "I don't give a fine fig what these people think!" he said, waving his arms. The women gasped and began whispering behind their hands.

"Well, I do! And it's my family's property that we're talking about. How do I know I can trust you if you go in there alone? What's to keep you from having the man sign the deed over to you instead of me?"

Boone grimaced, reached in his back pocket, and started to draw out a photo.

"Oh no! We've been down that road. You can't keep me out of this establishment!"

"What in tarnation is going on out here?" A large man dressed in a blue-checked shirt and dirty white apron stepped out of the bar room door.

They both spoke at once: "I'm here to pick up a deed!" Fuming, their gazes met.

Boone continued, "What she's trying to say is that *I'm* here to pick up a deed you've been holding."

"Oh, yeah?" said the man, with one raised eyebrow. "Who's it for?"

Boone paused, at a loss. Mindy stepped forward, shoving him aside with her elbow. "I'm Mindy McCorkle come to pick up a deed left to me by my uncle, Walter Larby." She gave Boone a triumphant smile. "We received a letter saying my uncle had died, and that a Mr. William Kirby was holding the deed to his property for us here at the saloon."

"Yeah. Old Walt. Left it here for you quite a while back. Come on in."

Boone reached to grab for Mindy, but she jerked past him and followed the big man into the saloon. It was a dark place. The small gas lamps had not been lit, and the only light came from the front window and the open door. The owner skirted tables with padded chairs pushed underneath and led them to a stained oak bar.

He turned to face Mindy. "I thought a lot of your uncle. Hated to hear when he got so sick. Then he came in one day and asked me to hold a deed for his sister. I was starting to worry that no one was coming." He went around to the back of the bar. "Hang on a minute, I gotta find the dad-blamed thing."

"That's no problem at all," Mindy said smugly.

When she turned to Boone, she noticed a man sitting at one of the tables with his head slumped onto his arms. A bottle and a glass rested near his head. Peanut shells were scattered over the rest of the table. Her eyes turned sad. "Oh, look. Poor man. I wonder what's wrong with him."

Boone rolled his eyes. "We've got to get you out of here."

"I'm not going anywhere and that's my final word on the matter!"

Boone's eyebrows lowered and he shook his head. "You are one unique item, little lady." He removed his hat and rubbed his head. "I don't know how I'm supposed to put up with this foolishness."

"There is no need to," Mindy said, raising her voice. "Leave me alone!"

The barkeep rose from behind the bar with a sheaf of papers in his hand. "There's a letter for you, too," he said. "I sure am sorry."

Mindy turned. "The undertaker said you took care of the funeral arrangements as well, Mr. Kirby. I'll be paying you back for that." She dug into her reticule.

"That's not necessary. Walt was a friend." The man took off his hat. "He was a friend to a lot of people here in this town. A real generous man. My girls all loved him."

"How sweet you are for saying so!"

"I'll just bet they loved him," Boone said under his breath.

Mindy whirled. "What do you mean by that? Are you slandering my uncle?"

Boone turned to the bartender. "We'll take that deed off your hands now."

"Not until I pay him for the funeral!"

Music started plinking in the background. A piano player was limbering his fingers and dancing out a few notes on the keyboard in the corner.

"It's time to go," Boone said.

Just then, a tall, silver-haired lady sashayed down a stairway at the side of the saloon. She watched the couple argue for a minute before saying, "She don't like you, cowboy. Maybe you'd like to find someone else to spend your time with." She winked.

Mindy couldn't help but note the undertone to the suggestion. Her back stiffened and her fingers fisted. "He absolutely would not!"

Boone glanced down at her. His eyes widened.

"Can I buy you a drink?" the lady purred, with all her attention focused on Boone.

"I'm sorry, ma'am. We're not staying that long." He smiled at Mindy, and then glanced back at the voluptuous woman. "Maybe some other time."

"Oooh . . . you would, wouldn't you? You just can't ever remember that little wife of yours, can you? Maybe I should go back over to the store and tell her what you're about!"

"I've told you before, don't you worry about my wife!"

"Somebody needs to," Mindy replied, with a lowered voice. She pulled money out of her purse and laid it on the polished surface of the wooden bar. "There," she told the man behind it. "There's thirty-five dollars."

"Now, let's get out of here," Boone said.

"I'm not going anywhere with you!"

"Well, I say you are!"

"And I say she's not." It was a male voice. Mindy and Boone turned to see Lucas standing in the doorway. The sunlight made a halo around his blond head and his tall shadow lay across the floor of the bar. His face was cloudy with rage. He spoke straight to Mindy. "I've been hunting you all morning. And I find you in a saloon? With him?"

Chapter Twenty-Three

Mindy blushed red as Lucas stomped into the barroom. She was embarrassed over such a display, even if there were only a couple of observers.

"It's not *a* saloon, Lucas," Mindy said, controlling her temper as best she could. These two men drove her up the wall! "It's *the* saloon. I came to collect the deed my uncle left to my mother. But I don't see why I should have to explain things to you, or inform you of my comings and goings."

"I would have been happy to accompany you. There was no reason for you to . . . disturb . . . Boone with this mission. It doesn't look right for a young lady to be out with a married man."

Mindy bristled. "And why should it be any of your business who I spend time with? You've asked to court me, not control me!"

*

Boone's ears perked up. So, they were a pair, now. She hadn't mentioned it. On the other hand, she didn't seem too happy about the situation. He smiled.

"I apologize," said Lucas. "Of course you're right. But I wish you would consider your reputation."

"What reputation?" Mindy demanded. "I don't know the people of this town. They don't know me. If they take my actions in the wrong way, I'm sorry, but that doesn't stop me from doing what needs to be done."

Boone agreed. Mindy never cared for propriety when she had made up her mind about something. He nodded his head, continuing to smile. Then he spoke. "I can see that Lucas has

things well under control. I can leave you in his competent hands."
Then, just to be evil, he said to Mindy, "Thanks. For everything."

Confusion settled on Mindy's face and Lucas flushed. Boone smiled even wider. "I guess I'll see y'all around."

*

Mindy watched Boone exit the bar, still puzzling over his last remark.

"What, exactly, did that mean?" Lucas demanded.

"I haven't the slightest idea."

"It's time to get out of here." Lucas took Mindy by the arm and almost dragged her from the establishment. Once they were outside, she jerked her arm away.

"What are you doing?"

"I'm trying to take care of you!"

"Well, stop it! I've had people taking care of me all my life! I've made it this far on my own and I reckon I can make it the rest of the way!" Mindy's eyes were glowing. She had worked herself into a fine lather. "Furthermore, if you continue to treat me like a child, I will have no choice but to think there is too great a disparagement in our ages! Perhaps I need to look for someone closer to my own age!"

"No, no, now, Mindy. Let's don't go that far. I'm just worried about you, is all," Lucas said, seeming to realize that he'd pushed her to the wall. "You have to look at it from my side." He reached for her hands, but she jerked them away.

"I suggest you look at my *backside* while I walk away!" Mindy roared. She left Lucas standing open mouthed on the boardwalk.

*

May 25, 1880
　Dear Melinda,

I am writing to you as I sit in the parlor, looking out the window. The flowers are blooming in abundance and there is a pleasant breeze blowing. It is truly lovely here and I wish you were home to see it. With each passing day, I worry more about you, and despise my decision to allow you to travel alone. What was I thinking? I pray that you are well.

The boys are good. I had a note from their teacher last week, saying that all but one are passing their courses in a fine manner. I suppose you can guess who happens to be the odd man out. Yes! Quinn! He is determined not to do his studies. The boy will be the death of me.

Your sisters are well and they each send their love. Little Sophie kisses your picture each time she visits and says she will kiss *you* when you return!

Gertrude Winegartner was married two weeks ago. She was beautiful in a rose satin gown and white veil. I think she and Robert will be quite happy together. That reminds me to tell you that Richard Peters has been by several times asking about you. If I didn't know better, I'd say he was sweet on you! You might consider giving him a chance when you return.

Edward Hardy took a case of the grippe two weeks ago and was in bed for six days. He had a fever most of the time. I had Bet take some chicken soup by. I know you would want to hear of it.

Mimmer Haygood got mauled by a threshing machine Thursday last. The physician is not sure if he will live or die. His wife would appreciate prayers on his behalf, I'm sure.

There also was a fire in the Town Hall not long ago. A gas pipe of some sort burst, but it was extinguished quickly enough that the structure remains largely intact.

In regard to the property, please take care of this issue as soon as you are able. I would love to see you home! Luther Mills said he heard unsettled land in Kansas is selling for three to five dollars per acre! Please be careful whom you do business with. The world is full of unscrupulous men. And women, for that matter.

Elizabeth asks for you frequently. If you have a moment, please write to her.

I pray for you daily.

I can think of nothing more to write at this time, but shall write again soon. You have my heart until I see you again. Until then, I shall remain,

Your Loving Mother,
Sordie McCorkle

*

September 15, 1879

Sordie,

I am sorry to leve you in such a pickle, what with having to take care of the property this way. I relize you are not a spring chiken any more and hope that the treveling has been easy on you.

You will find that Tipton is not a bad place. I heve enjoyed my time here imminsly. I have made good friends that I will miss derely. With luck, they will miss me as well.

I no this letter may upset you, but do not be dismayed, for I have made piece with my God and an redy to go if needs be.

You will find the homeplace easy. It is four miles out of town on the west road. There is a large bolder by the house for it was too large to be moved.

You are welcome to all I own. I hope that you or the children will come to love it as I do. I have spent many yers in hard work to see it to this point.

Trudy Mae is buried in the yard out back underneth the oak tree. I loved her well and now I can see her agin.

Plese do not be sad. All my love. I am now and will forer remain,

Your borther,
Walter Shotgun Larby

*

Mindy sat on the bed after she had read both letters, overcome with homesickness. Taking out a lace-edged hanky, she dabbed at the tears that freely flowed down her face. Poor Uncle Walter! She wished the family had been notified of his sickness so that someone could have been with him at the end. She made up her mind to go take a look at the property, rather than sell it outright. She needed to visit the home, touch the things, and see Aunt Trudy Mae's grave.

Having made up her mind to her next course of action, she was about to lie down for a nap when there was a knock on the door.

When she opened it, she was surprised to find Lucas standing in the doorway, his hat in his hand. "Mindy, please don't send me away," he said. "I've thought about my actions today, and I deeply regret them. I hope you will forgive me and give me another chance." He looked at her with hangdog eyes.

Mindy sniffed. "I'm not sure, Lucas. I'll have to think about it."

"That's fine! Think all you want. But I've had an idea. I figure you'll be wanting to go and see that property you have now, and I thought perhaps we could go together and take a proper picnic lunch."

Mindy paused. She did need to visit her uncle's home place, there was no doubt of that. She put one finger to her lip and peered at Lucas. "Do we understand that I am in control of my own life?"

"Yes, ma'am! I stepped out of line and I know it." Lucas truly appeared miserable. "I care for you, Mindy. I'd like a chance to show you."

He looked so sad and sincere that Mindy's heart couldn't help but thaw. She'd spent an age with him on the road and she knew in her heart he was a good man, if a little zealous at times. Besides, he might be the only hope she ever had of settling down.

"All right, then," Mindy said.

"Fine! I know you'll be happy with this decision. I'll have a buggy ready for us in the morning!"

When Mindy would have closed the door, he continued to stand there. "Yes? Is there something else?"

"Well, I wondered if you might join me for supper again?"

Mindy smiled inside. This was a new feeling and it was dangerously heady. "No, I think I will retire early this evening. It's been a stressful day." She glared at him.

"Yes, yes. I understand. May I ask one more thing? Why did you change rooms? I told you I would take care of the expense. I only want the best for you, Mindy."

"And make me indebted to you? *No*, thank you!"

Something in Lucas's eyes flared but was soon quenched. "As you like it. I will see you first thing in the morning."

Mindy closed the door, leaned against it, and breathed an exhilarated sigh. A man! Following her to apologize! Who would have ever thought!

Chapter Twenty-Four

Boone's sister, Becky, pulled up at the old home place. She helped Terese down from the wagon and entered her mother's house. The large receiving room was bright and cheerful, in part due to the late afternoon sun gliding through the windows. White wallpaper covered the walls with a brown, repeated star motif. The wood trim was painted a cheerful yellow, and mauve drapes with tassels hung from the two tall windows. Family photos lined the walls: black and white pictures of stern-looking people. A faded landscape painting hung over an ornate fireplace.

"Mother?" Becky called.

Terese didn't wait for an answer but ran through the house, hollering, "Nonny, Nonny!"

Mrs. Boone came out of the kitchen wiping her hands on a dishtowel. "Hello, you two! What a nice surprise." She swung Terese onto her hip. "How's Terri today?"

"She's fine, Nonny," Terese said with a giggle.

"Mother, please. It's Terese."

"You may as well give that up, Becky. This little girl is going to be known as Terri." She looked at the girl in her arms. "Aren't you?"

"Uh huh!"

Mrs. Boone set Terri down. "Myrtle has her pups in the kitchen, you want to go look at them?"

"Yes, *ma'am!*" the little girl said with a huge grin.

"Well, go on then, but be gentle."

Terri nodded and skipped into the kitchen.

Becky leaned forward and gave her mother a peck on the cheek. "How has your day been?" she asked. "Because mine has been *very* interesting."

"Really? How so?"

"Terese and I saw Gary at the general store today. He has evidently given some young woman the impression that I am his wife." Becky smiled in a crooked way. "Now, why do you suppose he would do a thing like that?"

"I don't know," said her mother. "But I've had the feeling he had a girl on his mind. This *is* interesting."

"She's a sweet little thing. Nice as she could be. But I got the impression there was a lot more going on there than was being said."

"I assume she's new in town," Mrs. Boone said with a speculative gleam in her eye. "I bet she doesn't know a soul . . . We should invite her to lunch."

Becky's eyes widened. "Oh, mother. Do we dare?" There was a tremble of excitement to her voice.

"I don't see why not. It's simply the courteous thing to do."

Becky threw her arms around her mother. "Sometimes I am reminded all over again how much I love you!"

"Oh, hush that up. Now go get me some paper and a pencil and I'll write the note right away, before I have to get back to supper."

"And I can deliver it in the morning."

"Good. Let's get this out of the way and then you can help me peel potatoes. The Hortons are coming for supper and you know how that man eats!"

*

Lee and Rich Byler were crossing into more familiar territory. It had been a hard, long ride and they had covered over ninety miles in three days, avoiding the towns of Great Bend, Pawnee Rock, and Burdett, for fear of their names being broadcast.

They were only a few miles from home, headed for a small, ramshackle spread just beyond Dodge City. One brother suggested a saloon stop to celebrate their victory, before they had to report the death of their two siblings to their mother.

Both boys knew their mother would take it hard, and they weren't looking forward to telling her. Now that they were getting close, any stop they could make would have seemed like a good idea. The opportunity to buy a few drinks and show off their newfound wealth was something they couldn't resist. With a population of just over one thousand people, Dodge City was a boomtown, and the boys hoped they could ease past without anyone giving them a second glance.

They clicked up the dusty, crowded Front Street of Dodge City, throwing dirt behind them. Small kids came out and ran behind their horses, playing a dangerous game of seeing how close they could get to the horses' hooves.

As they traveled closer to the stockyard, they were forced to ride through a herd of beeves that had been brought in for sale. The Bylers shoved at them with their boots as they passed, urging their horses forward and cussing at the cowboys who were leading the longhorns.

Once past the cattle, the brothers were able to set their horses at a small gallop as they passed several businesses on each side.

The town was constantly growing and it was a common thing to see several buildings with scaffolding. Here was everything a family could want or need. A general store *and* a mercantile competed for the citizens' business. A democratic newspaper, the *Ford County Globe*, was on the right, as well as a variety theater, the Granger State bank, and the Ford County Courthouse. On the left were a hardware store, the Dodge House Hotel, and a second variety theater. Among it all were saloons, dozens of them. It seemed that the primary entertainment of the city was drinking, and this was before passing into the "wrong" side of town where the brothels and more seedy taverns lay.

The boys halted and swung down from their horses in front of a place known as Peacock's Saloon. Tying their horses to the hitching post out front, they stomped into the relative darkness of a noisy oasis.

Lee and Rich stood just inside the doors and gazed around the room. It was filled with cowboys who were flush after a long cattle drive and intent on spending their wages having a high old time. In the corner, a piano player and a bass player pounded out a cheery tune that had several of the men dancing. Their partners were women of every size and shape, all wearing heavy makeup and big smiles.

There were no empty tables, so the boys walked over to the long, ornate bar and ordered whiskies. Without a second glance, the bartender poured each man a glass. When he would have taken the bottle, Lee made a motion. The bartender shrugged and set the bottle down. The oldest Byler laid a large bill on the polished flat surface. "Don't let us run dry," he told the man.

Lee turned his back to the bar and hitched a foot on the metal pole running the length of it. "Well," he told his younger brother as he gazed around the room, "look at all these pretty women. And they're ours for the choosing. Which one do you think pleases you?"

Rich smiled and glanced over each woman in turn. "I think the little redhead suits my fancy."

"That's fine. I like the big girl, myself." They both grinned and downed their drinks. After a couple more, they were feeling like they could fly.

"Well, brother," said Lee. "I've looked at your stinking face all I care to. I'm going to find me some female companionship. You look after yourself."

Rich nodded and watched as Lee cut in on a man dancing with a large framed woman with brown, teased hair. For a moment it looked like the man might cause trouble, but when he saw the darkness in Lee's eyes he backed down.

Rich ambled over to the card tables.

Both felt like they were finally living the good life.

Chapter Twenty-Five

The next morning, bright and early, Mindy dressed for the picnic and trip to her uncle's homestead with Lucas.

She was still reeling from the idea that a man—any man—would seek out her company. It had been years since she'd had attention from the opposite sex and she loved every minute of it. In her heart of hearts, she occasionally wished that the object of affection might be someone other than Lucas, a dark man perhaps, but that was impossible.

Despite the fact of his marriage, Mindy was drawn to Boone in a special way. With a sigh, she determined to put those feelings to rest and spend the day enjoying Lucas's company. If he was seriously interested in a long-term relationship, she was willing to give it a go.

A knock at the door startled her from her reverie. She answered it to find Boone's wife, Becky, standing in the hall.

"Hello," the young woman said brightly. "I hope I'm not calling too early."

"No," Mindy replied. "As a matter of fact, I was preparing for a ride in the country."

"Then I will only take a moment of your time." Becky handed a note with flowery script over to Melinda.

"What is this?"

"It's an invitation to lunch with me and my . . . Mrs. Boone. We'd love to have you join us, if you could. We thought since you're new to town, you may not have had the opportunity to make the acquaintance of many women. One can always use the company of women, especially in a foreign place." Becky smiled so brightly that Mindy couldn't help but smile back.

"That's so kind of you!"

"Not at all. If you can make it, we'll have lunch tomorrow at eleven o'clock. I will come 'round to fetch you before that."

Mindy bubbled with excitement at the thought. The company of women! It had been so long since she'd had female conversation, she worried she might have forgotten how to do it. She said as much to Becky.

"I can imagine, being cooped up on that stage for so long with only men! But I'm sure we'll all get along famously. And you'll love my . . . Mrs. Boone."

As they spoke, Lucas walked up, and Mindy had to make her goodbyes, with the promise of seeing Becky on the morrow.

She was giddy with the idea. When Lucas took her arm and wrapped it around his, she didn't mind in the slightest. It would be a wonderful day!

*

The ride to Walter Larby's home wasn't a long one, but it provided the couple time to talk and get better acquainted. Mindy learned Lucas had been a captain in the War Between the States. He had fought on the side for states' right, and since her own relatives had also fought for the Confederacy, this news gave Mindy some relief. He told her anecdotes regarding his time in the military, and their shared laughter put Mindy more at ease. She found that she was quite comfortable in his presence.

Upon arrival at the farm, Mindy was pleasantly surprised to find a tin-roofed, saltbox house with an "L" added. It was painted white and had a porch that wrapped around two sides. There was a slat-board fence surrounding the home and a tall oak tree stretching its arms over the whole. In the rear of the house. a second oak tree stood sentinel.

"Oh, how quaint!" Mindy exclaimed. "The setting is picturesque!"

"It is a lovely home," Lucas said, pulling on the leads to the horses.

He stopped the wagon, set the brake, and then helped Mindy down. Mindy skipped up to the front porch, where a wicker swing was hanging. She plopped down and swung her legs back and forth, gripping the ropes with her two hands.

"Can you imagine coming home to a place like this?" she said. "The wheat growing in the field, cattle grazing, chickens running about in the yard with the children, and the heady smell of supper coming through the open windows?"

"I can imagine it," Lucas said with all seriousness.

Mindy didn't pause. "Oh, I'm so sorry that my aunt and uncle didn't have children. It would have been wonderful to grow up here!" She looked out over the property, taking in a deep breath of fresh air. "It's truly lovely!"

"It is. How many acres?"

"The deed said one hundred and forty-two. I'm not sure about the boundaries, though."

"That can easily be established," Lucas replied. He sat on one of the porch rails and crossed his arms. "There's more to see, you know."

"Yes. I know. It's just that the home seems sad in a way, like it's waiting for someone new to come along and take care of it." Mindy sighed. "But there's nothing we can do about that, is there? I suppose we should see the rest." She hopped off the swing and stepped toward the front door. "Oh, it's open." She peeked around the door. "I hope no one has been using the house."

Lucas pulled Mindy back and stepped in front of her. He pulled his gun and eased his way in. Mindy followed close behind.

"Hello?" Lucas called. "Anyone here?" A lonely house echoed back. He peeked into a couple of the rooms and then slid his pistol back into its holster. "It's okay, probably just the wind."

Mindy glanced around the room. The wooden floors showed signs of wear and the furniture was a bit threadbare, but she thought it looked like heaven. She felt a peaceful sensation, like she was coming home.

As she walked through the house, Mindy touched different pieces of furniture, picked up knickknacks that were displayed on the fireplace mantel, and admired the needlepoint work in handmade frames on the walls. "This home was loved," she said. She ran a finger across an occasional table by the wall. "Everything is covered in dust." She smacked her hands back and forth. "But that's easy enough to remedy."

"Let's see about the kitchen arrangements," Lucas said, turning toward that opening. They entered into the hub of the family home and found a simple handmade wooden table and chairs, and a dry sink with a pump. A cast iron stove sat in one corner.

Suddenly, out of a pie safe against a far wall, there came a large dark shadow, moving at the speed of a locomotive. Mindy screamed and jumped up on a chair. Lucas dropped into a low stance and pulled his gun. The culprit was a raccoon! It perched itself on the dry sink and looked at each of them in turn, showing no fear.

"Do something! Do something!" Mindy gestured wildly to Lucas.

"It's just a raccoon," Lucas shouted.

"Get it out! Get it out!"

Mindy's screaming upset the animal, and it paced back and forth across the counter, watching her with a steely gaze.

Lucas snuck around the perimeter of the room and opened the back door. He snuck back and jumped toward the creature. "Yah! Yah! Get on out of here!" The raccoon sat back on its haunches and glared at him. "I said, 'Yah!' you evil thing! Get out! Shoo!"

From her perch, Mindy put her hands to her mouth and began to snicker. Lucas looked up at her and then set his mouth. He ran at the creature, waving his arms and shouting. Finally, the animal jumped to the floor and waddled out the back door at a sedate pace.

Lucas turned to Mindy, triumphant. She couldn't help herself, but burst out laughing. A moment later, Lucas began to laugh as well. He walked over to Mindy, grabbed her around the waist, and picked her up. He turned a couple of times as they laughed, sharing a delightful moment.

Chapter Twenty-Six

They picnicked on a blanket under the tall oak tree. Lucas had brought a basket prepared by the hotel kitchen staff that included cheese, ham, chicken, biscuits, and fruit.

Mindy finished eating and lay back on the blanket to look at the sky. After a moment, she said, "Did you ever make pictures from clouds when you were small?"

Lucas lay down beside her. "Of course I did. I'm still pretty good at it . . . see?" He pointed with one finger. "There goes a cannon." They laughed. He reached to take her hand and Melinda let him hold it for a moment before she sat up, realizing it would be easy to give him too much encouragement when she still wasn't sure what she wanted. "It's been a sweet day, Lucas," she said. "Thank you."

"It's been my pleasure. I think this house has potential." He looked deep into Mindy's green eyes. "I'm interested in buying the farm."

"Really? I hadn't considered that, but it would be perfect for you. I can see you here."

"I can see you here, too, Mindy." He took her hand again. "It would be perfect for *us*. I hope you'll think about it. You know my intentions."

Mindy pulled her hand back and looked away. "It's awfully quick, Luke. I need time."

Lucas smiled. "Well, Lord willing, we have plenty of that." He lay back and stared up at the blue sky above them. "Look, there goes a general."

Mindy looked down at him and smiled. He was such a kind man, and it seemed he really cared for her. She could do worse. Of course, at this point in life, there was the possibility she could do without. She noticed his well-combed blond hair and couldn't help but think of Boone and his unruly mass of brown locks.

With Boone, she wanted to run her fingers through it; with Lucas, she was satisfied to see it from a distance.

"What are you thinking?" Lucas asked.

"Just silly thoughts. Nothing that matters." They were quiet for a few minutes before Mindy asked, "Why me, Luke?"

"What?"

"Why me? I'm sure you've known lots of women in your life. Why me? Why now?"

"I don't know, exactly. There's just something about you that makes me smile. You warm my old, cold heart. I had stopped believing that was possible, Mindy." He gazed at the house and field. "And I can see you as a wife. You've proven you can handle tough situations. You may be a little tenderhearted, but I admire that. You're brave . . . you're beautiful."

Mindy snickered. "I'm afraid it is love, because they say love can be quite blind."

"No, you are beautiful, Mindy. You've just never been around a person who can see it like I do."

"Well, I've been around a lot of people, Lucas, but I've never been accused of being beautiful. You may be too old and senile for me!"

The rest of the afternoon passed in like fashion. When he dropped her off at her hotel room door, he asked her to supper again, but she declined.

"Let's take it slow, Luke," she said, before she smiled and closed the door.

*

The next day was filled with activity as Lucas set out to have the property surveyed and Mindy prepared for her visit with the Boone ladies.

She decided to walk to the general store to buy new gloves, and couldn't help but notice the townsfolk decorating the streets for the upcoming Independence Day. A large banner was being raised over the dusty main street: *July Fourth Celebration!*

"A lot of excitement about the holiday," she commented to the proprietor.

"Oh, yes," said the gray-headed man behind the counter. "We do the Fourth up right. We have a barbeque and a dance, and games, and contests of skill. People come from miles around to join the celebration." He smiled with obvious pride.

"I'd love to see it, but I don't think I'll be here that long," Mindy murmured.

"It's worth staying for," he said with a wink.

*

Boone rose later than usual. He was disgruntled and irritable. Ever since the incident with Mindy and Lucas in the bar, he couldn't get the two of them out of his head. It was funny how Mindy always made him want to hit something. This time, he was afraid it was Lucas. He finished his morning chores with a scowl.

Boone had finally heard from the managers of the stage line. He had been encouraged to find a couple of cowboys to join him, and then head off in search of the money and the Byler brothers. He had plans to head into town as soon as he cleaned up after his morning meal.

At the breakfast table, his mother was impatient. "Gary Boone! Why do you have to wear your boots into the house! I swear, you'll be the death of me, yet."

Boone looked up from his eggs and ham. "What did I do this time?"

"Those boots are filthy, and every time you wear them in the house you track mud and dirt to kingdom come."

Boone leaned back in his chair. "Let me get this straight. You want me to take off my boots before I come in the house?"

"Well, it wouldn't hurt you!"

Boone glanced around. Something about the house seemed different. Everything sparkled and gleamed. His mother always kept a tidy home, but it looked as if she were preparing for a visit with the queen. "You having company today?"

"I am, and your dirty ways don't make it any easier." Mrs. Boone was scurrying around like a beaver. She came to the table and picked up his plate.

"I wasn't done with that yet."

"Well, now you are." She scraped the leavings off into a slop bucket and plunked the plate in a dishpan full of soapy water. "Don't you have something to do? I don't need you underfoot today." She seemed nervous for some reason. Boone shook his head. Women!

"I'm planning to head to town here in a minute. Will that suit you?"

"That'll be just fine! Now get up from the table, and get on with yourself. I need to get that cleaned up." Boone slid from his chair as she began wiping the spot where he'd been eating. "Go on."

"Yes, ma'am." Boone shook his head again.

As he walked toward his bedroom, she called, "And you'll need to find something to do in town for a while!"

"Yes, ma'am!"

Boone washed up and put on a fresh shirt. Once outside, he saddled his horse and climbed up. It was a beautiful day. The blue sky stretched from horizon to horizon and was full of puffy white clouds. If only his attitude was as clear and bright.

He set off down the road toward town, trying to get a certain girl off his mind.

*

Becky picked Mindy up at ten forty-five with an excited smile. "Are you ready?"

"Yep. Just let me get my reticule." Mindy glanced around the room to make sure she hadn't forgotten anything. "Okay, I guess I'm ready," she said as she pulled on her new gloves. Her luggage had arrived, so she'd been able to don one of her nicest dresses. She wore an afternoon ensemble of a long blue skirt with a slight bustle, and a white blouse with a square neck and ruching.

"Then let's head out!"

The two women climbed into the buckboard and began the short trip to the Boone home. As they neared the homestead, they saw a lone rider approaching at a slow gallop. As he drew closer, the girls saw that it was Boone.

Mindy nodded, but Becky waved and smiled from ear to ear. Boone stared, openmouthed.

Chapter Twenty-Seven

Becky hopped down from the wagon. "Let me take you in and introduce you to . . . Mrs. Boone . . . and then I'll come back and see about the horses."

Mindy wore a faint smile. She twiddled her hands.

Becky smiled. "Are you nervous? Don't be! We won't eat you."

Mindy ran her eyes over the traditional farmhouse. It was a white one and a half level, with a wide veranda. Several trees competed to cover the house with their leafy, green branches. Mindy sighed. So this was where Boone was raised. It looked like home.

Mrs. Boone came out onto the front porch, waving. "Halloo!" she called. "Come on in!"

Mindy glanced at Becky, who smiled again and nodded. "I promise. No biting."

As she stepped onto the porch, Mindy immediately felt at peace. Mrs. Boone was warm and welcoming, and greeted her with a familial hug. "I hope you won't mind," she said. "It's just that I've been excited to meet you!"

"Me?" said Mindy.

"Yes. I've heard good things about you, and I have a feeling we're going to get along famously. Come on in!" She led the way into a comfortable house, and gestured at her surroundings. "It's not much, but it's where we live. While you're here, I insist you make yourself at home."

Mindy studied the older woman. She was dressed for company, but in a simple afternoon frock. It was a green on green dress with a large bustle. The sleeves had been rolled back and the front was lightly dusted in flour.

"I see you've found my secret," Mrs. Boone said, as she followed Mindy's gaze. "I don't believe in servants. I do my own cooking and cleaning. As a matter of fact, I'm running a bit late with our meal. Do you cook?"

"I can find my way about a kitchen."

"Good! Then you'll come help me!" Without another word, Mrs. Boone spun around and headed toward the hub of the house. "We're having chicken and dumplings—I hope you like them. My broth is calling me; I need to drop in the dumplings. And if you don't mind, I'll let you peel tomatoes and pour the glasses."

Mindy sighed with relief. Activity! She didn't know what she would have done if she'd had to sit on a starched sofa making inane conversation!

Mindy jumped into the work and soon she and Mrs. Boone were chatting like old chums. Becky arrived, carrying fresh flowers from the garden. She gave them a good soak and began arranging them in a vase for the table.

"Of course, I meant to have all this done before you arrived," Mrs. Boone said, blowing a stray wisp of gray hair from her forehead. "But the best laid plans . . . "

"I understand," Mindy said. "My mother is the same way. She tries to make everything perfect for company but ends up forgetting the most important things . . . Oh! I don't mean that you . . . "

Mrs. Boone laughed. "You're exactly right. The house got a good once-over, but here I am asking our company to help in the kitchen!"

"I love it, actually. These tomatoes look wonderful and the dumplings smell delicious."

"Mrs. Boone makes the best dumplings in Marion County," Becky said with pride.

The trio made a good team and soon the ladies were seated at the dining table. Mrs. Boone said grace and they began to eat.

Mindy made yummy noises, and both Becky and her mother grinned. "I told you they were the best dumplings!"

"The green beans are delicious, too!" Mindy said. "How long have you been here?"

"Oh, about twenty years now, I suppose. We moved here

when Gary was about nine or ten. Becky wasn't even born then."
Suddenly, Mrs. Boone seemed to realize what she had said and
looked up to find Mindy's curious gaze on her. "Of course. She
wouldn't have been. She's years younger than Gary. I suppose she
would have been . . . born . . . later. Don't you think, Becky?"

"Yes, ma'am. Certainly. I certainly agree." Becky coughed.
"Would you care for more tea, Mindy?"

Mindy's gaze traveled from one woman to the other. Something
had made the two strangely uncomfortable all of a sudden. She
placed her hands in her lap while they struggled with words.

"I think Becky was born . . . near here. Weren't you, Becky?"
Mrs. Boone was saying.

"Yes. Quite close. Yes." Becky coughed again, a choking sound,
and then said, "Mindy, won't you have more dumplings?"

Mindy's eyebrows arched, but she said nothing.

The meal passed without further disruptions and afterwards,
the ladies adjourned to the living room.

"Tell us more about you, Mindy," Becky said. "All we know
so far is that you were on the same stage as Gary when it had the
wheel accident that left you all stranded. He came in with a head
wound but had little to say about what happened or the people
with him. You know how men are."

"Well, there's not much to tell. I'm from a small town in Mississippi.
I live with my mother and three brothers. I have three sisters who are
married and I have three adorable nieces and nephews."

Mrs. Boone smiled at Becky and then said to Mindy, "I'll bet
you're good with children. You have a very pleasant way about you."

"Oh! I love children. I've always wished for my own, but things
have never quite worked out in that regard. I've never found a
man that was suitable . . . or that found me suitable." Mindy
laughed. "I'm getting used to my 'old maid' status now."

"But you're still a young thing! If you don't mind me asking,
how old are you?"

"Twenty-three. Long on the shelf, I'm afraid."

"Not at all! As a matter of fact, I think I know someone who may be interested." Mrs. Boone met Mindy's gaze. "Someone close to you."

"Yes. Lucas seems to be a fine man. We've spent quite a bit of time in each other's company. I like him very much."

"Lucas?" Becky and Mrs. Boone said together. "Who's Lucas?"

"The man who . . . " Mindy paused. "But then, who were you talking about?"

Mrs. Boone looked at Becky and then straightened her shoulders. "Mindy, there's something you should know. Becky and Gary are not married."

Mindy gasped. She'd heard of these things before, but had never thought to run across it!

"No, no!" Becky said. "I'm married, but not to Gary. He's my brother."

Mindy glanced from one woman to another. Her red face flushed even more. She felt like the biggest sort of fool. "You mean . . . ? I'm not sure I understand."

Mrs. Boone looked at Mindy with gentle eyes. She stretched out a hand. "I don't know why Gary would tell you such a thing. But there's something else you should know. As his mother, I feel I know my boy very well, and I think—"

Mindy stood up. "I'm sorry. I don't mean to be rude, but I'd like to go now."

Mrs. Boone stood. "But, Mindy, please let me finish."

"I think I've heard enough. Perhaps I do understand . . . Boone is not married to Becky. The child I saw with him is not his own. He lied to me."

"But don't you understand there has to be some reason? Boone—Gary—is not a liar by nature."

"I think I understand that, too." Mindy said. "He didn't want to tell me that he wasn't . . . " She looked at Becky. "I'm sorry. I'm feeling ill. Could you take me home?"

"Of course." Becky stood up and headed for the door. "It'll only take me a moment to prepare the wagon."

Mrs. Boone started to speak, but Mindy cut her off. "I think I'll wait outside if that's all right. Thank you for a pleasant lunch." Mindy held out her hand in a formal fashion.

Mrs. Boone sighed. "Mindy, this is not at all how I had hoped today's luncheon would go."

Mindy continued to stand with her hand out and Mrs. Boone accepted it. "Thank you for joining us, Mindy. I hope to see you again soon, perhaps under better circumstances."

Mindy turned and headed for the front porch. The air there felt stale and hot. She fanned herself with one hand, feeling a bit nauseated. As she waited for Becky and the wagon, she saw a rider approaching and could tell by the way he sat the horse that it could be no one else but her Tormentor.

Boone stopped the animal in front of the house, slowly dismounted, and took off his hat. "Mindy."

Mindy nodded, but said nothing. She stared past his head into the distance, willing Becky to hurry, with her hands clasped tightly in front of her.

Boone stepped up onto the porch. He held his hat in his hands, circling it. "I came to talk to you."

"I have nothing to say to you, Gary Boone."

"But Mindy, I didn't mean for things to get so . . . "

"Well, they did, didn't they?"

Becky arrived then, tearing around the house with the wagon.

"If you'll excuse me?" Mindy marched down the stairs, lifting her blue skirt as she went. She climbed into the buggy, saying only, "Please take me home."

Becky looked back at Boone with daggers in her eyes. He shrugged and then threw his hat to the ground.

Mindy maintained her dignity until she arrived back in her hotel room. There, she finally broke down, throwing herself on the bed and weeping until she had no tears left to cry.

Chapter Twenty-Eight

When Boone stepped into the house, his mother was waiting. "See what you've done!"

"What *I've* done? She was fine until she came to lunch with you two!"

"Gary Boone, you will not raise your voice in this house, and you certainly will not raise your voice to me. That girl will go home and cry her eyes out because *you* lied to her, not because we revealed it."

Boone's shoulders slumped. "Well, what am I supposed to do? She's being courted by a rich dandy who can offer her anything she wants. What can I give her?"

"See there. I knew it! You care for her."

Boone slapped his hat against his leg. "Heck yeah, I care for her!"

"What do you intend to do about it?"

Boone looked up into his mother's gaze. "Do you think she'd listen to me if I tried to explain?"

"Probably not. But it sure wouldn't hurt to try. I like that little girl, Gary. Now, you go get her."

Boone's eyes turned hard. He set his hat back on his head with a determined shove. "Yes, ma'am!"

*

Mindy had dozed off. She awoke to a loud banging on her door. "What is it? Who's there?" she called. She wiped her eyes and realized how puffy they were. She was so tired of crying!

"It's me, Mindy! Open the door!" It was Boone's voice.

"What do you want?" She hollered, tossing her leather journal at the wooden door. "Can't find any children or animals to torture? You decided to come and torment me?"

"No! Mindy, I'm not trying to torment you." There was a dull thump on the door, as if he were leaning his head against it. "I don't rightly know what I'm trying to do. But I need to talk to you."

"Well, talk!"

"Through the door?"

"If you've got something to say, say it. I'd just as soon not look at your face!"

"All right then." There was a long pause.

"Well? Do you have something to say, or don't you?"

Boone exhaled. "Min, are you happy with Lucas?"

"What?" Did she hear correctly?

"Does he treat you right? Are you happy?"

Mindy thought his voice sounded muffled. She rose from the bed and walked nearer to the door. "Yes, he's good to me. Why?" A small sparkle started in her heart.

"No reason, I guess. I just wanted to be sure."

Mindy jumped as a fist hit the door halfheartedly.

"I want to know if he ever treats you bad. You deserve a good man, Min."

When she opened the door, Boone almost fell in. He looked pitiful and she knew for a fact she didn't look any better.

"Oh. Hi there, Min." Boone took his hat in both hands and started circling it. "I'm sorry to barge over here like this, but I was worried about you. You know, after the way you left the house."

"You were worried about me?"

"Of course I was. I could see you were all upset." Boone rubbed his head. "I wanted to say that I'm sorry. That I lied to you. At first it was just to shut you up . . . you being a pain and all on the trail. You understand. But then I ended up with my britches hitched on my own pitchfork. I didn't know how to fix things without looking like a fool."

Mindy crossed her arms and cut her eyes at him.

"Like now, I reckon." Boone shook his head. "I ain't never talked to a real lady, Min. I don't know the flowery things to say or the right words to use. I'm not like Lucas, all spit-shined and polished."

"Why on earth would you want to be like Lucas?" Mindy asked. If she didn't know better, she'd think Boone was trying to tell her he was jealous. Imagine! *Two* men. She struggled to keep a smile from her face.

"Never mind. The thing is . . . I care for you, Mindy. I've never cared for another woman the way I care for you. I'd like a chance to show you."

Mindy almost swooned. She stood for a moment with her mouth open. "But . . . Boone, I thought . . . "

"I told you I'm not too good with talking, Mindy." Boone stepped forward and placed one hand on either side of her waist. He pulled her toward him, and before she knew what to expect, she was lost in his kiss. A long, dreamy, searching, foolish kiss. When he set her back, she stood dumbly. She couldn't speak or think. Her eyes had glazed.

Boone started to grin. "I guess Lucas doesn't kiss you like that, does he?"

Mindy drew back, realizing how forlorn she must have looked, now that the kiss had ended. She spat, "It's none of your business what Lucas does or does not do!"

"I'd say it is!"

"Now how do you figure that?"

"I just told you that I care about you. What else do you want? Flowers? Hard candy?" Boone kicked the doorframe. "I knew it was stupid coming over here like this. I told ma that—"

"What?" Melinda paled. "Gary Boone, did your mother set you up to coming over here?"

"Well, it was her idea, but—"

"Then you go back and tell her it didn't work! I don't know what pleasure you get in tormenting me, Gary Boone, but I don't care for it. Not one bit!"

"I told you, Mindy . . . " But the door slammed in his face.

Mindy jumped again when a loud bang sounded on the other side of the wall. She waited a few moments and then opened the door and looked out. Boone was gone, but there was a huge fist imprint in the wall.

Chapter Twenty-Nine

Boone secured one man to help with his mission and tried to think of a second. His thoughts kept coming back to Lucas. Admittedly, part of the reason would be to keep him away from Mindy for a few days.

He found Lucas in a saloon on Main Street, flirting with one of the barmaids. His temper soared. Before he knew what he was up to, he had Lucas in a headlock in the middle of the dirty street.

Lucas gave him an elbow to the ribs, and with a great, "Uumph!" Boone lost his hold. The two men circled each other but Lucas jumped first. He grabbed Boone by the waist and threw him to the ground. Boone reacted by throwing a roundhouse punch to Lucas's jaw. The blow knocked Lucas aside and he lay there panting and holding the side of his face. He started to rise.

This time, Boone jumped, throwing Lucas back to the ground; he gave Lucas several sharp blows to the face before the two were broken apart by a sheriff who had come running when the commotion started.

"What in Sam Hill is going on here?" he demanded. "Don't you two have anything better to do than scare the women and children of this town? I ought to lock you both up for ignorance!"

Lucas pointed a dirty finger at Boone as he rubbed his jaw. Blood trickled from his nose and mouth. "He started it."

"I don't care who started it. It's finished now! Go on!" The sheriff was a no-nonsense older man. He had graying hair with a cowlick at the temple. His cheeks were flushed as he chastised the men.

Lucas eyed Boone with hostility, but Boone shook the dirt off his pants and turned to leave. He gave Lucas a last look. "Treat her right, Lucas, or I swear I'll come after you."

"All right, all right. We've said all we need to say. Now, go on!"

The sheriff gestured with his hands.

Boone had taken three steps in the opposite direction when he was tackled from behind. Lucas threw him to the ground and began pummeling his kidney.

The sheriff stepped in again. "That's it! You're both headed off to jail. I can see you ain't got this out of your system yet. We'll just give you two little ladies time to think about it." A deputy arrived, grabbing Lucas, as the sheriff helped Boone to his feet. He was favoring his right side.

The steel doors clanged shut and the boys looked at each other from adjacent cells.

"Are you happy now?" Lucas asked.

"Naw, I ain't happy," Boone said. "Not when I see you cozying up to some other girl while you've been courting Mindy! She deserves better than that!"

"It's none of your business what she deserves! That's between her and me!"

"I'll say it's my business! You're not the only one who cares for her!"

Lucas's mouth dropped open. Then he paused and a smile started, lifting the corner of his lips. "Well, ain't that just too bad, friend. Because we know who it is she's spending her time with, don't we?"

Boone lunged at Lucas through the bars but the blond man backed away, still smiling.

"You better watch your back, Lucas. I'm waiting to see how you treat her."

Lucas lay back on the cot in his cell and tipped his hat down over his face. "Well, watching it ain't the same as living it." He chortled. "I think I'll just get me some shut eye while you stew on the matter."

Boone started to punch the wall, but instead sat down on his own cot and gently tested the side of his stomach. It felt like Lucas had ruptured something!

*

Mindy heard about the fight at the mercantile later that morning. She marched down to the jailhouse with eyes that sparked.

The two boys woke when they heard a familiar voice: "I tell you I want to see them, and I want to see them *now!*"

The sheriff mumbled something under his breath, but soon preceded Mindy down the hall to the room where the boys were now standing.

"I just want you to know that Boone here started the whole thing, Mindy," Lucas said quickly.

"I don't give a fig which one of you started it! How dare you both shame me in front of the people of this town! Fighting like dogs over a bone! How'd you think this would make me feel?" She stared at each one in turn. She had her hands pressed firmly to her hips and looked magnificent. "I hope the sheriff leaves you locked up for a week!"

Mindy turned to Boone. "And what do you think your mother will say when she hears of this? I imagine she's going to be right proud of her son, then, huh?" Lucas laughed and she turned on him.

"And I thought better of you Lucas Wilhite! Don't you *dare* laugh!"

Lucas sobered immediately. "But Mindy . . . "

"Don't you 'but Mindy' me! I've had it. I don't want to be seen with either of you! Think about that!" Mindy whirled and stomped out of the room, skirts flying.

The sheriff lingered in the holding room a bit longer. "Hoowhee, boys! She is something else. Good thing neither of you decided to tangle with *her* in the street today!" He laughed the whole way back into the office.

Chapter Thirty

When Boone and Lucas were released from jail, they went their separate ways: Boone to prepare for his trip, Lucas for a bath and shave and then to visit Mindy to try to make things right.

Boone quickly found another man to complete the threesome that would be going after the Byler brothers. Both men traveling with him were older and more than qualified. One, Jake Myers, could track a ghost across a wide open plain. The other, Micah Powers, was trail-hard and one you'd be glad to have in your corner in any fight.

The boys were loading up outside the general store, when suddenly Boone cursed, throwing his pack onto the horses' back. There was no way he could leave without trying to say a word to Mindy. But why did he care? What was it about her that had him so enraptured? She wasn't the prettiest thing he'd ever seen. She sure wasn't the daintiest. And she cried at the drop of a hat. But he'd never known another woman that would pull a gun on a man! Or travel alone across the country. Or chew him to high heaven. Except, maybe his mother. Dog gone it! He hated seeing that similarity!

These feelings were foreign to him and he didn't like them. His ma might call it love. Boone spat in the dirt. Love! Regardless, he soon found himself marching angrily to the hotel. He pounded on Mindy's door.

*

"Good heavens!" Mindy said. "What is it?" When she opened the door to find Boone standing there, in his two-day-old clothes, with two-day stubble, and a swollen, black eye, she told herself he looked like a filthy beast. Her heart didn't agree. "What on earth could you want?" she demanded.

"I reckon I came to say goodbye. I'm headed out to find the Bylers and won't be back for a while. I just wanted to . . . " Boone twisted his hat. " . . . tell you, I guess."

Mindy stiffened and crossed her arms over her chest. "And I'm supposed to care?"

"Naw. I reckon not." Boone paused. "But I thought—heck! I don't know what I thought." He stared at her face. "I guess I'm sorry for acting the way I did. I'm sorry you got mad about the fight."

"You mean, you're sorry for the fight," Mindy corrected.

"No, I'm not sorry for the fight. I'm just sorry you got all up in the air about it. I guess I'd do it again, given the chance."

"What kind of apology is that? You never cease to amaze me, Gary Boone. You expect me to forgive you when you're not even sorry?"

"I'm not trying to *apologize*!" Boone shuffled from foot to foot. "I'm just sorry you got mad, is all!"

"Humph!" Mindy said, tightening her arms. She couldn't help but consider the dangerous mission he was about to undertake. After a lengthy pause, during which the two stared at each other, Mindy asked, "How long will it take to get to Dodge City?"

"Dodge City?"

"Yes. While we were walking those days, Byler mentioned the city a couple of times. Made me think he was from around there. He kept saying that there were tall beers waiting on him in Dodge City. Didn't you hear him? It was before we found the water."

"No! I don't make a point of listening to shiftless, whining, worthless men."

"Well," Mindy said, giving him a pointed look. "I guess that's part of my problem. I do."

Boone's face hardened. "All I got to say is that we're leaving. I don't know when I'll be back. If you leave town before I . . . " His hat went round and round in his hands. "I guess it was nice knowing you, is all!"

"Humph!" Mindy said again. "I'm not sure 'nice' is the word. But it was interesting, I'll give you that!" Then she pictured Boone riding out of town and into trouble, and she leaned forward, grasping the doorframe. "You know those Bylers will be ready to fight anyone who tries to take that money. You'll be careful, won't you?"

Boone raised an eyebrow. "Does that mean you care a little?"

Straightening, Mindy recrossed her arms. "No more than I'd care about anybody else headed off into danger."

Boone studied her eyes for a moment and then softened his voice. "To tell the truth, Min, I'll be more worried about leaving you here alone, than going after those fellows."

Mindy's resolve melted a bit. What was it about this man that made her heart skip? Well, except that he was fine to look at, and was the sort of man that could handle most any emergency or situation. And there was the way he often looked at her with those black eyes that made her knees grow a little soft.

And of course, there was his kiss. "I appreciate your concern. But I'll be fine. Thanks, though, for caring."

"That's just it, Min. I do care. I care a lot. More than I want to, to tell the truth. You got me so tore up, I couldn't hit the ground with my hat in three throws."

Mindy laughed. "Oh, I doubt that. I've seen you with that hat."

"Yeah," Boone said, meeting her smile. "I guess you're right."

"When are you heading out?"

"We're saddled up and ready."

"Oh!" Mindy looked toward the window and then back. "Now?"

"Yeah. I've been sitting too long as it is, waiting to hear from the stage company. The trail's long cold by now. I appreciate the tip about Dodge City."

"That's all right. So, you're leaving *right now*?"

"That's what I said. Why? Do you need me to stick around?"

"No, of course not! I just didn't think you'd be leaving . . . so soon."

"Yeah. If I miss you, I wish you luck back in Mississippi. It was nice knowing you, Mindy. Real nice."

"Yes, Boone. It's been . . . It's . . . " Before Mindy knew what she was doing, she threw herself onto Boone's chest, surprising them both. His arms instinctively came around her and his head bent to lie against her hair. She enjoyed a quiet moment and the pleasant sensation of being within the circle of his arms. "Take care of yourself," she said. Her voice caught.

"Hey." Boone set her away from him, looking into her green eyes, which were glassy and bright. "I'm going to be fine."

Mindy reached out and touched the wound at his temple. "Yeah. You can't be hurt, huh?"

"All I can say is that I promise I'll be back. If you're still here, you'll see me again."

Mindy collapsed against him. She wondered what her mother would think of her, being so familiar with a man, but decided she didn't care. There was something about Boone that made her do stupid things. And there was something odd about herself, so that she didn't give a hoot.

"Boone?" Mindy said, looking up into his eyes. "Would you kiss me again before you go?"

Boone looked shocked, but smiled and said, "I sure will. I'd be proud to." Taking her face gently in both palms, he looked dead into her eyes. She took a step forward, until their lips were almost touching and their breaths met. "You make me crazy, Melinda McCorkle. But I'm finding that I seem to like crazy." He closed the distance between them.

Boone's lips were gentle as he brushed against hers in a sweet brief kiss. Mindy sighed as he pulled away. But he took another step closer. One strong hand went around her waist, while the other slid to the back of her neck, underneath her unruly mass of curls. He kissed her again. This time the kiss was deeper, more passionate, and Mindy leaned into it. In a moment they each turned greedy, seeking the comfort they might find in the other. It was a kiss that said what words could not. When he raised his head, Boone still held her near, breathing hard. "You make me crazy enough to eat the devil with horns on, Min."

Mindy smiled. "You make me crazy, too." She pulled away. "But I'm not sure it's a good kind of crazy. I can't think straight when I'm with you."

"Then don't think at all. Come 'ere." Boone pulled her to him and kissed her again, gently. When he sat her back, he heaved a deep breath. "Well! That'll give me plenty to think about while I'm gone."

"Yeah. You're leaving."

"Sorry, Min. I . . . "

There was a sound of boot steps approaching. Boone gave Mindy another quick peck and let her go. Not before Lucas had seen it, though. "Step aside, Boone!"

*

Boone turned to face Lucas. He was conflicted. He knew in his heart that Lucas was a good man, and he couldn't help but feel that Mindy might be better off if she chose the other fellow. But he'd be horse-whipped before he walked away and let it happen. "I'm leaving, Lucas. I came to say goodbye to Mindy."

"Looked like you were doing more than saying it," the blond man said.

"I stole a kiss, is all. Don't let it worry you."

Lucas glanced at Mindy. Her face was flushed and she wouldn't meet his eyes.

"Mindy, I came to ask you to have lunch with me. I wanted a chance to apologize for yesterday."

"No, I don't think so, Lucas. I'm sorry. I'm not very hungry," Mindy answered.

"Perhaps supper, then?"

"Maybe. I don't know, Lucas. I'm very confused at the moment."

Boone settled his hat on his head. Confused! Hot dog! He could leave with a good conscience. He felt that if she were still here when he got back, he'd have a fine chance at courting her. If not, he'd chase her all the way down to Mississippi. It wasn't that far away.

"Well, I'm off," he said. He nodded at Mindy. "You take care of yourself while I'm gone."

"I'll take care of her." Lucas answered for her.

Boone stared hard at Lucas. "That's what I'm afraid of."

*

On the trail later, Boone played the scene over in his head. The other two fellows riding with him kept trying to make conversation, but he wouldn't have any of it. His mind was miles away. For the first time in his life, he was thinking about marriage.

Chapter Thirty-One

June 23, 1880

Dear Elizabeth,

How I miss you! I must apologize. I never truly appreciated your friendship until my journey. Having to do without our visits for an extended period reminds me what a good friend you've been.

Oh, the things I need to share! This has been the most fascinating, horrifying, infuriating, extraordinary, wonderful trip. I have had such extreme highs and lows that I wonder I do not get seasick!

Please do not tell mother, but on the last portion of our stage ride here, we were left stranded by a broken wheel. Together with six other persons, all men, we set about walking toward our destination. It was abominably hot and tiresome—I can't fully express the situation in mere words.

Along the way, we were set upon by thieves—who killed three of our men!—and we discovered that one of the men traveling with us was part of the terrible gang. He had been sent along as a scout I suppose. I was lucky to escape with my life. It was only owing to the bravery of the last two men that I am alive to write you this letter. I know you will worry, but I am fine. Above all, keep this information to yourself.

Allow me to tell you about the men. One is a tall, fair-headed, older man named Lucas Wilhite. He was a captain in the War Between the States, and is very brave and charming. We have been keeping company since our arrival in town. I can imagine how you read that with surprise! After all these years of waiting for someone to notice me! (I didn't realize I had to simply leave my hometown to make it so.) Lucas is purchasing my uncle's farm, and I expect him to ask me to marry him and settle there. I am considering it. He is a fine, stable man and I believe he would make a good husband and father.

The other man is also tall—taller than Lucas—and he has dark hair that is rarely combed. His name is Gary Boone, and he has the most amazing black eyes. We fight like brother and sister at times, and he can be most frustrating, but there is something about him that calls to me. He has recently professed his concern for my welfare, and possibly, that he has feelings toward me as well. Can you imagine? Two men who have found *me* interesting? My head aches with the thought.

Elizabeth, I will tell you a secret, but only upon our childhood honor of keeping certain things close to heart—I have allowed Gary to kiss me! More than once, I'm afraid. How was it, you ask? Heavenly! Though I suppose all kisses are heavenly as far as I know, but since these were my first, they seemed . . . special.

Boone is a marshal, and has a most dangerous job. He recently left Tipton in search of the murderers who robbed us. I pray for his safe journey and return. Along with the men riding with him, of course.

You would like Tipton, dear friend. It is larger than we are used to, and has everything a body could ask for. If I decide to marry Lucas, I believe I could be happy here.

Mother wrote me about a few of the things happening back home. I hope that Edward Hardy is recovering from his bout with the grippe. I can only imagine what torture he is putting his wife through, she being so dainty and kind, and he being such a brute. Owing to my brothers, I have learned how pitiful men can be when they are sick!

I trust Mr. Haygood is recovering well from his threshing accident. Poor man! Mother also mentioned Gertrude's fine wedding. I am glad she finally got Robert to the altar!

As another surprise, Mother commented that Richard Peters has been asking about me. Can you imagine! He hasn't given me the time of day since we were pups!

As to my return, I expect that it will be farther away than expected. There are so many details to work out. Not the least of which is my relationship with Lucas!

Until we can meet again in person, I remain forever,

Your dearest friend,

Melinda

*

June 23, 1880

Dear Mother,

I am writing to tell you what has happened since my last letter.

You will be happy to know I have found a potential buyer for Uncle Walter's farm. As a matter of fact, I mentioned the man to you in my most recent letter. He is the Civil War captain, Lucas Wilhite.

There are many details to attend to; therefore, I do not know the date of my departure.

I thank you again for allowing me to undertake this journey. It has been most enlightening. Hope all are well. I send kisses.

I think of you fondly, and will do so until we see each other again. I remain,

Your loving daughter,

Melinda

*

Melinda had been invited by Becky to attend the weekly Tipton Women's Club gathering on Thursday. She excitedly prepared for the visit and planned her outfit carefully, finally choosing a light green day dress with a small bustle and ruffled collar.

Mindy met Becky outside the meeting site, the First Congregational Church. The two talked in animated fashion about what had been going on since they last saw each other. Mindy suspected that Becky wanted to ask about what had happened when Boone came to talk to her, but the subject was never brought up. After all, it was a girls' day!

Inside, Becky introduced Mindy to some of the more active members of the club: Mrs. Celia Logan, the chairperson, Mrs. Zora Ponder, the secretary, and Miss Merle Lacy, a newcomer with great enthusiasm. Mindy tried to remember all the names, but they soon began to blend together.

The meeting started and Mindy listened as the ladies talked about their plans for the upcoming Fourth of July celebration.

"We've sent the announcements to our neighboring towns. I took care of that last week, so we should have plenty of company," Mrs. Ponder said.

"And I've heard back from Senator Watson and Governor Terry. They both plan to be here and have agreed to honor us with speeches for the occasion," said Miss Lacy.

"Delightful!" Mrs. Logan clapped her hands. "Now, what's next? Oh yes! Steven Knight has agreed to provide two cows and a pig for the barbeque, and Bill Daves of the fire squad has agreed to obtain the fireworks."

The plans continued and Mindy grew more excited. She didn't know if she would still be in town for the event, but it certainly sounded exhilarating!

Becky spoke up. "Mother and I, and Mindy here, will sew and hang the bunting." She smiled when Mindy looked at her openmouthed. "You can sew, can't you?" she whispered.

Mindy smiled and nodded, thrilled to take part in the festivities and have something to do. She needed to keep her mind off a certain man.

Chapter Thirty-Two

Rich and Lee Byler were knee-walking drunk. They exited the Peacock Saloon and lurched into their saddles. The time had come for them to face their mother. A bright, full moon lit their way as they eased toward home.

As they pulled to a halt in front of the old homestead, a run-down mud and frame shack, Lee hollered out, "Ma! We're home!"

Rich lolled in his seat, grasping at the pommel with both hands before falling sideways from the horse.

Lee started laughing. "Hey, Ma!" he shouted. "Ma!"

A light flickered behind one of the shuttered windows and grew steadily brighter. In a moment, a tiny, gray-headed woman opened the door. She wore a nightgown, and carried an oil lamp. "What is it? What's the racket about?" Her voice was shrill.

Lee hollered, "They're dead, Ma. The boys are dead . . . " He looked at Rich on the ground and began to laugh. "And we're dead . . . drunk!"

The woman stepped farther into the yard. "What do you mean, they're *dead*? Where are your brothers?" Her voice rose. "You tell me what you mean, boy!"

Lee put on a sober face. "They killed 'em, Ma. Tweren't nothing we could do. It's just me and Rich now." Lee climbed down off his horse and walked toward his mother, but she waved him off.

"Where's my baby? Where's my Roger?"

"He's gone, Ma. That's what I'm saying. Him and Ben were shot dead."

The woman threw her head back and began to keen. She collapsed in a heap and put her head to the ground. "No!" she cried. "Not my baby!"

"It were Ben, too, Ma," Rich said from his position in the dirt. He had seen the wisdom in staying where he was; his legs didn't seem to be working. "But they died brave. You'da been proud of them."

Rich's mother never heard. Her sorrow was overwhelming. The boys looked at one another. They'd never heard a sound like the one their mother made. It was eerie, and echoed in the dark night, chilling the bones.

Lee began to cry. He staggered to where his mother sat on the ground. Moving the lamp aside, he knelt with her, putting one hand on her back. "It'll be all right, Ma."

The woman rose up and smacked his hand away. She stared him in the eyes and spat, "How could you let this happen? Better you die than my Roger. He was just a boy."

"What?"

"You heard me. You boys have always been worthless. Good for nothing but shooting! But my Roger was an angel. How could you let something like this happen to him?"

Lee sat dumbfounded. He looked over to Rich, who was passed flat out on the cold, gray dirt of the front yard. He opened his mouth to speak, but his mother drew back an arm and slapped him with all her might.

"I don't know where you'll be sleeping tonight, but it'll not be in my house! And you can drag your sot of a brother out of my sight!"

Lee reached for her, but his mother staggered to her feet, pitched into the house, and slammed the door. When her wailing began again in earnest, Lee walked over to his brother and kicked him in the ribs.

"Ugh!" cried Rich. "Whaddya . . . whaddya . . . doin'?"

"Get up! I ain't carrying you. We gotta bunk in the barn, so get up!"

"Wait," Rich said. "Gimme . . . just a minute."

"Take all the time you need, brother." Lee wiped his face, then turned and stumbled off in the direction of the lean-to barn, leaving his brother where he lay.

Chapter Thirty-Three

Lucas took Mindy to the 49ers Restaurant for lunch on Saturday. It was two crowded rooms with cloth-covered, square tables and a long counter. The top half of the walls were painted a bright pink, with white wainscoting beneath. Colorful paintings in wooden frames decorated the space and lent it a homey atmosphere.

Once Lucas and Mindy were seated, a harried lady in a flowered apron came by the table and plopped down menus.

Saturdays:
Son-of-a-Gun Stew
Fried liver and onions
Calves' feet
Roast mutton

Grits and gravy
Fried potatoes
Fried eggs
Vegetables (whatever's fresh)

Vinegar pie
Molasses pie
Fried fruit turnovers

$1.25 a meal

"Oh my," Mindy said with a laugh. "I love molasses pie *and* fried turnovers! Can we start with dessert first?"

Lucas took her hand across the table. "We can do anything you want."

Mindy's smile slid from her face as she slid her hand from his. "Lucas, don't . . . "

"No, no. Let's don't talk about anything negative today. We've worked out our differences, and I want to stay on the right course."

"It's just that—"

"Mindy, I don't mean to be rude, but I'd like for you to let the past go. The fight was unexpected yet unavoidable, in my opinion. When I saw Boone with another woman, I became enraged." Mindy's eyes widened, and he continued, "I couldn't stand the thought of him deceiving you. I spoke to him, and he attacked me. There was nothing I could do. I hope you understand."

"He was with another . . . ?"

"Yes, dear. He was in one of the saloons."

Mindy put her hand to her mouth. She sat back in her chair to absorb the information. Had Boone kissed another girl the way he kissed her? Were his kisses given away so freely? The thought of his lips touching another's quelled her spirits.

"I hope I haven't disturbed you, Melinda," Lucas said with a concerned look.

"No. Of course not," Mindy said, flapping her cloth napkin onto her lap. "I've simply never thought of Boone doing that sort of thing."

"You'd be surprised what men will do. After serving in the army, I can tell you that men always amaze you. When they should be brave, they cower. When they should be honorable, they are base and dishonest. Now, what will you have to eat?"

Mindy studied the menu before she said, "I think I'll have the mutton, please."

"The liver and onions are very good. I would recommend that. As a matter of fact, I think I'll order it for both of us. You will be very pleased."

When the aproned lady came by, Lucas flagged her down. "We'll have two livers, please. Then give us each the fried potatoes and a helping of the vegetables—what are they today?"

"Parsnips."

"Wonderful. We'll have dessert afterwards." When the woman walked away, Lucas turned back to Mindy. "I think you'll be much happier with the liver." He smiled warmly.

Mindy folded her hands into her lap, and nodded.

Nearby, a ruckus started. A deliveryman was in a heated argument with the owner of the restaurant.

"Them's the prices they told me, them's the prices I go by."

"How can I make any money at these prices?" the bespectacled, whiskered owner said. "Twenty-seven cents for a bushel of potatoes! Sugar up to fifteen cents a pound!"

"There's nothing I can do about it, neighbor. I just deliver the goods."

The owner pulled some bills out of the cash register and handed them over.

"Since the gold rush, everything has gone up in price," Lucas said, shaking his head. "During the heyday, there were places where potatoes sold for a dollar and a half a pound. Eggs and oysters were a dollar each!"

"You don't mean it!" Mindy said.

"I do. Greed will do strange things to people."

The meal came and the pair ate in relative silence. Mindy found that she didn't have much to say. But the liver and onions was good, she had to admit.

"Have you made a decision about the property?" Mindy asked, as she stopped to take a drink of tea.

"Yes. I'll buy it, if you'll take three dollars an acre. That's over four hundred dollars for a little girl like you."

Mindy bristled. "First of all, I'm not a little girl. Secondly, I'm selling the property for my mother. And finally, I will not take three dollars an acre. I have been told property here sells for much more than that."

"You'll not get more in this economy," Lucas blustered.

"Then I'll hold it," Mindy replied.

"Now, wait a minute. I have every intention of buying that property, Melinda. How much do you want per acre?"

"Four and a quarter."

"You must be joking!"

Mindy stared into Lucas's face.

"Fine. Fine! Four dollars an acre, then."

Mindy paused, and then nodded. "I think that will be sufficient."

"You know that's close to six hundred dollars? What will your mother do with that kind of money? Will you see any of it?"

"Why? Does that matter?"

"No, of course not. I just wanted to see if you would be well-situated," Lucas said. "I wouldn't want to worry about you. I've told you I care for you, Melinda. I mean it."

Mindy bowed her head. "I'm not sure about anything right now, Lucas."

"I understand, but I plan to purchase the property either way. I have hopes of us living there together as man and wife. Without you, that farm is next to worthless."

"Then I would not recommend you purchase it at this time, Lucas. I . . . "

"Forget I said anything. We've got plenty of time. We'll go by the bank when we leave here. I'll transfer the funds and you won't have to worry about that anymore. Only if—"

"No more talk. Let's have dessert."

Chapter Thirty-Four

It was less than a week before the Fourth of July. The ladies of the Tipton Women's Club had been active little bees. Holding another impromptu midweek meeting, they reported on the activities lined up for the celebration.

Merle Lacy bubbled. "Everything is set for the rodeo. It's to start at six p.m. We already have several cowboys signed up, and I'm sure there'll be more. It should be thrilling!"

Some of the other women in the room tittered, and began whispering.

"Now, quiet down, ladies, please," said Mrs. Celia Logan, the chairperson. "I know we're excited, but we have much to do. Let's stay on track. I think we should go over our items in the order the events will take place. Perhaps it will be less confusing." She looked at a pile of papers on her podium. "That means we start with the parade. That's you, Ivy Faith, isn't it?" Mrs. Logan turned to a middle-aged woman with brown hair and a dimpled face, sitting in the second pew.

Standing, the lady said, "Yes, Celia. The parade will begin at ten o'clock. That should give our visitors time to arrive and get settled. We will meet with all the participants at the north end of Main Street to line up and then we'll proceed south." She smiled sweetly. "We have cowboys, kids on horseback, three motor carriages, the Tipton General Band, and assorted wagons that will be gaily decorated."

"You've done a fine job coordinating that, Ivy," Mrs. Logan said. "Next, is . . . Mary Hubbard and Brenda Murphree. You ladies are taking care of the games of skill?"

Those two ladies stood and looked at one another. One gestured for the other to do the speaking. Mary began, "We have decided on a number of games for the afternoon. So far, we have a pulling contest, a greased pig, a greased pole, an egg toss, a frog toss, a three-legged race, a horse race, and an Old Timer's horse race, for those men who are fifty and above." She nodded to the other ladies as they made exclamations. "People can sign up before each event for fifty cents and we'll have cakes and pies donated as prizes for the winners."

"You heard that, ladies. We need those cakes and pies. We want to have lots of winners," Celia said.

Mindy leaned over to Becky. "Does it matter what kind of cake or pie it is?" she whispered.

Becky shook her head.

"Then I'd like to make a couple of apple pies, if you will allow me to use your kitchen."

Becky took Mindy's hand and gave it a squeeze. "We'll do it together!"

About that time, they heard a loud "harrumph" from the front of the room.

Becky stood. "I'm sorry. We were discussing pies." She looked around at the happy faces. "Mindy and I have been working on the bunting and have it almost ready. We'll begin decorating downtown tomorrow or the next day, and yes, we'll take all the help we can get!"

She sat down and Mindy gave her a nod. "Good job!"

Celia voiced her encouragement. "Next, let's see . . . oops! I forgot our noon meal, but that's being handled by the men and only deserves a brief mention." She paused and gave a knowing look to her audience. The ladies all laughed. "Yes, we'll be following up behind them all day! We'll need food items to go along with the meat, so I expect everyone to bring a dish and a dessert. And you know the men will forget things like plates and cups and things of that nature . . . "

"Or won't want to use them!" someone shouted.

"I expect you are right," said Celia. "I'd like a couple of women willing to oversee that task. Barbara? Isn't your husband one of the cooks that day? Then we'll put you down. Select some women to help you, please." Celia waited for a nod from that lady. "The speeches by our prominent men will take place after the games. Then, last but not least, will be the fireworks display, and the men have that handled, as well. Our job will be to pray. Let's hope the whole town doesn't go up in smoke!"

This comment was met with many chuckles. Celia waited until it subsided before speaking. "Is there anything else? If not, I expect everyone to help out somewhere. And this meeting is adjourned." She slammed a gavel.

Outside, Mindy greeted the women again, pleasantly surprised that she could put names to many of the faces. As they walked toward the hotel, she said, "This is going to be such fun! I can't wait to see the frog toss!"

Becky said, "You'll love it! It's not as easy as it sounds."

They walked on for a few moments before Mindy said, "I admire Mrs. Logan, the chairperson. She does a wonderful job of heading everything up."

"Yes," Becky replied as they crossed the dirt street, avoiding a couple of men on horseback. "She's been the chairperson for years. No one else would have the job. It's like trying to herd cats!"

They both laughed and then Mindy turned to her. "Let's have lunch together! It will be my treat."

"That sounds great, except for the treat part. I have to get Terese from a friend's, and then we'll meet you . . . at the hotel?"

Mindy nodded and they separated.

*

Lucas had agreed to take Mindy to the farm that afternoon to visit her aunt and uncle's grave. She wanted to have a quiet memorial service. When Becky heard about it, she offered to join them and bring Terese and her mother.

On the way, Mindy and Lucas chatted about the celebration. She encouraged him to enter the greased pig contest.

"Not me," he said with a chuckle. "I'm too old. I'll leave that to the young bucks. The horse race sounds interesting, though."

Mindy rejoiced. It had been a good day and she was happy with the world. The sun shone overhead like a blinding diamond in the sky. Though the day was cloudless and hot, riding in the wagon kept a breeze flowing against their faces.

"Have you thought any more about what it would be like to settle down and quit your wild ways?" Lucas asked, nudging Mindy.

With a laugh, Mindy said, "I've thought about it a great deal. Mother has been afraid for years that I would end up on the shelf like my aunt. I love the idea of having my own home and someone to look after. What about you?"

"I've been thinking about it a lot in recent days," Lucas said, with a quick glance to see Mindy's reaction. "I've been roaming for too long. I love traveling and seeing new things, but after a while, it's as the good book says—there's 'nothing new under the sun.'"

"I can just imagine a houseful of kids underfoot, little boys and girls who are constantly getting into mischief. My brothers and I were terrors growing up, but we had fun together. We played in the log pile and made our own whistles and rolled hoops, and were constantly playing tricks on one another.

"Sounds like you *were* a handful!"

"I suppose. But Mother handled it with great aplomb. Even without a father, we grew up terrified of our mother's wrath if we had gone too far."

"I was an only child. Your life sounds exciting."

"It was. I can't wait for a houseful of my own. Though my mother has warned me that things have a way of coming even and

I will probably be paid back for the woes I caused!"

"I've thought about children, Mindy, but decided I'm too old at this point. I like the idea of me and my wife working together side-by-side."

"But that sounds so lonely," Mindy said.

"Not if you have the right wife," Lucas replied.

*

At the gravesite, they were met by Mrs. Boone, Becky, and Terese. The little girl carried a large bouquet of wildflowers tied with a pink ribbon. Mindy was touched at the thoughtful gesture. Bending down, she gave Terri a kiss on the cheek and thanked her.

"That's all right," Terese said with a mature air. "We wanted to help your feelings."

"Well, you sure did. These are the loveliest flowers I've ever seen."

Terese smiled and then tucked herself behind her mother's skirt.

The small group gathered around the two silent graves under the oak tree. Lucas said a few words and then led a prayer.

Terese pulled on her Nonny's skirt. "Why is Miss McCorkle crying? Is she sad?"

"Yes," said Mrs. Boone, swinging the child onto her hip. "So we have to give her lots of love to help cheer her up. Can you help do that?"

The little mop nodded. "I like her."

"Me too," said Mrs. Boone. "Me, too."

Chapter Thirty-Five

Boone and his companions were on the trail of the Byler brothers, hoping to bring them in for murder and robbery. They had been hired by the stage company, and authorized by the marshals' office.

The men passed through lonesome gorges and wide open fields. They galloped past buffalo grazing in tall grasses and they scared rabbits from their happy warrens. They cantered through small towns, stopping only long enough to ask if anyone had seen the Bylers. When their questions were answered in the negative, they returned to their horses and flew back into the wind.

The men lived off beef jerky and dried fruit. They ate beans cooked slowly over an open fire with cornmeal cakes and coffee. At night they made their beds under a canopy of glittering starlight.

Micha, the oldest man in the group, had a beautiful baritone voice and his songs accompanied them wherever they went. In the dark evenings, when all was silent, his voice was a peaceful, dreamy background to the men's thoughts.

As the three men crossed the state of Kansas, Micah sang:

In a cavern, in a canyon,
Excavating for a mine
Dwelt a miner forty-niner,
And his daughter Clementine

Oh my darling, oh my darling,
Oh my darling, Clementine!
Thou art lost and gone forever
Dreadful sorry, Clementine

Boone, Jake, and Micah rode for four days before reaching Dodge City. Barreling into town, Boone gave a signal at the sheriff's office and the men stopped, hitching their animals to the post outside. They stretched, muscles aching.

The office was a frame building, like the others in a long row. The windows and doors were open to allow for circulation of air. Boone's boots echoed across the boardwalk and onto the wood floor of the office. "Hello?" he called.

A medium-sized man came from the back of the building. "Hello, yourself. How can I help you?"

Boone answered, "I'm Gary Boone." He gestured to the men with him. "This is Micah Powers and Jake Myers. We're looking for three men we think may be holed up near here."

The deputy held out his hand. "Bat Masterson. Good to know you." He nodded at Micah. "I think I know you."

"Yes, sir. I came through here last year. I found your town right hospitable."

"Glad to hear it. Not all the comments we hear about this place are good. My partner and I are trying to fix that."

At that time, another fellow came through the front door. He glanced past the men, speaking to Bat. "Everything's fine at the Lone Star. It was just a drunk causing a dustup. It didn't take much to put him back in his place." He turned to Boone and his companions, and then stuck out his hand. "Wyatt Earp."

Both of the deputies wore white shirts and dark pants. They had coal black hair and inset eyes. Both sported mustaches.

Boone and the men introduced themselves again, and then Boone came to the point. "We're looking for a couple of fellows by the name of Byler. You know 'em?"

Bat looked at Wyatt. "Yeah, we know 'em," he said. "Nothing but troublemakers, the lot. Not a single one out of the four is fit to shoot at when you want to unload and clean your gun."

"Well, there's just two now," Jake said. "Boone here had a shootout with them a while back, over a small thing like a stage purse. Two of the Bylers didn't make it. One of the others got shot up."

Wyatt laughed. "Can't think of a better bunch it could happen to."

Bat said, "Them and their maw got a little farm out past town about five miles. I imagine that's where they are. The oldest one, Lee, and one of the middle brothers, Rich, I think, were in town just a few nights ago. I guess they were celebrating their good fortune."

"Y'all feel like accompanying us out there?"

"I don't mind," said Bat, "but we need to leave someone here to mind the office. We got prisoners that have to be minded." He looked over to Wyatt, who nodded.

"I'll stay back this time. Wear 'em out."

Boone replied, "I *hope* they'll come in without a fight."

"Not those boys," Wyatt said. "And look out for the mother—she's as mean as the boys, if not more so."

The men exchanged glances. "Might explain a lot," Boone said.

Chapter Thirty-Six

The ride to the Byler farm took about an hour. The men stopped before they reached the house to reconnoiter and devise a plan. When they were approaching the homestead, they took in a peaceful scene. Since it was almost noon, there was a lazy curl of smoke arising from the small frame shack, evidence of a cook stove in use. Lee Byler was out behind the house chopping wood. The riders pulled up for a moment, allowing him to finish and load his arms. Micah, Jake, and Bat detoured to take positions surrounding the house. Then Boone rode into the yard alone.

"Lee Byler!" Boone shouted, as he stopped his horse in the dusty backyard. "You had to know we'd find you. I'm here to take you and your brother to jail for murder and armed robbery!"

Byler, with his arms full of wood said nothing, but his eyes met Boone's as if sizing him up for a fight.

"Call your brother," Boone ordered.

From the corner of his eye, Boone saw a movement at one of the windows. The barrel of a shotgun poked out. With a curse, he slapped his horse on the rump and took off just as the gun discharged, the shells missing him by scant inches. Lee Byler threw down the firewood and ran for the safety of the house.

Boone rode for cover. He stopped at an outcropping of rocks just to the side of the house, then caught Bat's eye and shook his head in disgust. They had figured it would go this way.

"Lee Byler! You and your brother are coming with me today, whether it's alive or dead. It's your choice!"

A voice shouted out the window. "Well, that's right neighborly of you folks! But I'm sorry. I believe we'll decline your fine offer."

A female voice hollered, "You're lucky I didn't kill you just now. I reckon you're the man that murdered my sons and shot up my boy!"

"There's no reason for anybody to get hurt. Come on out and let's settle this peaceably!" Boone hollered back.

"Byler! This is Bat Masterson, deputy sheriff of Dodge City. You boys have got more trouble than you can handle. You ought to come on out and save yourself some grief. Your momma don't want to bury no more boys!"

"Don't be talking for me, Sheriff!" the lady of the house shouted. "My boys ain't going anywhere. You just come on in here and try to take 'em!"

Boone inched his way across the rocks, sliding to Bat's position. "Do we go for the plan?"

Bat said, "Hang on a minute. We need to—"

At that moment, a hail of bullets passed over their heads, causing them to drop down. Bat reached up and removed his hat, fingering an inch-sized hole near the crown.

"Now, if they keep this up, they're gonna make me mad," said Bat, with a frown. He looked Boone square in the eye. "We go with the plan."

Boone raised one arm to signal the other two men. At the sign, Jake took off his bandanna and climbed back on his horse. He guided the animal to the blind side of the house, where he stopped and stood up in the saddle. Wadding the piece of cloth, he placed it in the ventilation hole for the stove. Then he rode quickly back to his position and ducked down.

After that, it was simply a waiting game. As smoke filled the house, the men could hear the occupants coughing and wheezing. Soon, the door opened and the two boys came charging out, guns blazing. Their mother followed, collapsing just outside the door.

Lee Byler carried two revolvers and was shooting indiscriminately. Rich followed, with his right hand bandaged and a gun in his left. He was having a hard time handling the weapon, but managed to fire off several shots. The Byler brothers ran for the barn, but Bat,

Boone, Jake, and Micah opened fire. Rich fell to the dirt and was still. Lee whirled and dropped low, firing at the rocky shelf where Bat and Boone were positioned. A bullet coming from the other angle tore through his arm. He grunted and fell back, dropping both pistols as he grabbed his wound.

Micah and Boone stepped cautiously away from the rocks and toward the last living Byler brother. Boone kicked the guns away and bent to help the man to his feet. As he did, bullets started to fly again. He heard a muffled grunt and spun to see that Micah was down. Boone plopped into the dust and spied Mrs. Byler holding a revolver in both hands. When the gun finally went *click, click, click,* Mrs. Byler crumpled to the packed clay with wrenching sobs.

Bat walked over and jerked her up by the arm. "I ain't never arrested a woman before, but I'll warrant today looks like a fine day to start!"

"My babies! My boys!" she screamed.

"Your boys got exactly what they deserved," Bat said with a growl. "And so will you." He jerked her over to his horse where he grabbed some rope.

Boone squatted to check on Micah. He looked to the other two men and cursed, shaking his head. "He's gone."

Jake bent to see about Lee Byler's wound. It was a through and through. "You'll live, more's the pity."

"You're all worthless pigs! You'll never get me to jail," Lee shouted as he was hauled to his feet.

Boone walked over and put the still warm nozzle of his pistol against Lee's temple. "We can make sure right now you never get to jail, if that's what you want."

Byler swallowed hard, his eyes darting between the gun and Boone. "Ss . . . s'all right. I'll go."

"I thought you might see it my way." Boone released the hammer and lowered his weapon. "Just remember you're outnumbered. Any crazy stunts and you won't make it to tomorrow. As far as I'm concerned, you wouldn't be missed."

Jake went to the barn and came out with three horses. He had them saddled and prepared for riding. Bat picked Mrs. Byler up and threw her onto the back of one of the plug horses. He had tied her hands together while she cussed him to heaven and back again.

Bat glanced over to Boone and indicated the woman with his head. "She's so mean, I think she'd fight a rattler and give him first bite."

"She's an evil one, that's for sure."

Boone stripped off his bandanna and tied it around Lee Byler's injury.

"Oh . . . I'm hurting bad," Byler moaned.

Boone balled his fist and punched Lee in the arm at the direct site of the bullet wound. He started to say something, but Byler passed out. Boone shrugged instead.

It took a while for the men to get everything handled. After removing the piece of cloth from the vent, Boone waited for the smoke to clear and then ventured into the house. He threw water on the fire in the cook stove and then searched the home until he found a canvas knapsack with the cash and documents he was after. Rifling through them, he saw pretty quick that part of the money was missing. He cursed again.

When he exited the house, Boone found that Jake had thrown Micah and Rich's lifeless bodies over their horses, and that both the remaining Bylers were bound and sitting on horses as well. Mrs. Byler continued to rant, her voice grating on the nerves as the men headed out of the yard.

*

When they arrived in Dodge City, Bat, Boone, and Jake swung down from their horses in front of the sheriff's office. They'd had all they could stand of Mrs. Byler and had a greater understanding of how the boys turned out as they did. Bat grimaced and said, "Maybe you boys ought to go ahead and take this she-devil on with you to Tipton."

"Sorry," said Boone with a half smile. "This is where her crime was committed. You know the rules."

Boone and Jake helped load Lee Byler and his mother into jail cells and then they took the two other horses down to the undertakers. They delivered the dead bodies and paid for them to be buried.

Then both boys went in search of a bath, a drink, and a bed.

*

Two exhausted men and one prisoner headed out of town the next day, after thanking Bat for his help.

"It was nothing," Bat said. "Part of the job. Y'all come back when you can enjoy yourselves. We got a nice little place here . . . most of the time."

On the trail again, the boys found they missed Micah's singing. They tried a halfhearted rendition of "Clementine," but let it go after a couple of verses. Most all they could remember was the chorus, and the singing made them miss Micah even more.

They traveled in silence after that.

Chapter Thirty-Seven

Sunday morning, the Fourth of July, 1880, dawned bright and clear. It was a perfect day for a celebration.

Visitors to Tipton started arriving by seven a.m., pulling their buggies and wagons into open areas, and tying their horses to anything that didn't move.

Main Street filled with tourists—they peered into shop windows and poured into the local eateries. Children galloped up and down the boardwalks, playing games and making new friends.

Morning services started at eight o'clock in the Congregational Church, and there was standing room only in the modest building.

Mindy sat in the fourth row with Mrs. Boone, Becky, and her husband, Neville, and little Terese. The pint-sized bundle was difficult to control this morning. She stood in the pew and turned this way and that, staring out the windows and the open church doors to the activity taking place just a few yards away. She pulled on her mother's sleeve, asking, "Mommy, where did all the children come from?" Her eyes glowed with excitement and wonder.

Her mother shushed Terri repeatedly, suggesting she would take the child out if she didn't behave, though Becky didn't seem to have the heart to carry out the threat. It was too glorious a day. The entire church was filled with a palpable sense of expectancy.

Members greeted each other with broad smiles and happy hugs. They sought out visitors, pumping hands and slapping backs, and when those gathered raised their voices in song, the rafters echoed with the sound.

*

Mindy and company exited the church building, saying their goodbyes and good wishes to the preacher and his wife. When they stepped out onto the boardwalk, their hearts filled with exuberance and pride. Red, white, and blue bunting hung from the storefronts all the way down Main Street. Flags were on display in every possible position, with their thirty-eight stars blazing against a canvas of blue.

Becky spoke the words Mindy was thinking. "It looks good, doesn't it?"

"I've never seen anything like it!" Mindy turned to Becky and grasped both her hands. She was even more excited than Terese! "And to think that we had a part! I'm so excited. What do we do first?"

"Well, unfortunately, among all the fun, we have work to do. I told Celia that we would volunteer part of the day as helpers. Otherwise, I don't think she would get a chance to enjoy herself at all. I hope you don't mind."

"Not at all! I'm thrilled to take part. We've never had anything this size in our little hometown back in Mississippi. Let's get started!"

Becky turned to Neville and said, "Last chance. Are you sure you don't mind watching Terese this morning?"

"I want you two to go have fun. Work hard, but have fun." He gave his wife a kiss on the cheek. "Terese will be fine. Between Nonny and me, she'll be spoiled rotten by noon." They all laughed and then Neville said, "We'll see you at lunch."

"Well then," Becky said, with a wide grin, "we're off to work on parade organizing. Pray for us!"

Mrs. Boone picked Terri up in her arms, and they both waved gaily as the two women headed up the street to where parade participants were staging. In the middle of a huge crowd of people, they saw the harried Celia Logan.

"Here we are. Ready to help!" Mindy announced as they walked up.

Celia turned and visibly relaxed. "Thank heavens! Would one

of you please go speak to those confounded cowboys and ask them to move their animals *away* from this area? We're already having complaints and the parade hasn't even started yet! Tell them to congregate over near the cemetery."

"Will do," said Becky, as she marched away.

"What about me?" Mindy asked.

"Could you keep an eye out for Ivy Faith? She has the list with the order of procession. And then go speak to the men with the steam coaches and motor buggies, and ask them to move a little farther down the street. We need to keep them separated from everything else—they're spooking the horses . . . and some of the people, for that matter."

"Yes, ma'am!" Mindy headed off toward the strange vehicles, excited to finally see one of the new fuel-driven, internal combustion wagons up close.

The morning passed in a blur. By the time the event started, the girls barely had time to run and seek a suitable spot from which they could watch the parade. The boardwalks were filled. There were even people perched on top of the buildings! Mindy took it all in with openmouthed wonder.

Several gaily decorated wagons came first, some promoting local businesses. Mindy and Becky laughed and pointed at a man riding in one of the wagons who was dressed as George Washington.

Next, the motorcars, with black smoke belching out from behind. The people watched in fascination as these new contraptions moved along at speeds of four to five miles an hour!

Then followed three wagons, which were decorated with the new bunting that the girls had made. In the first was the mayor of the Tipton, Reuben Lowe; in the second was the esteemed Senator Joseph Watson; in the third was the governor of Kansas, John Pierce St. John. The men looked fine and distinguished in their black cutaway suits and white shirts. The crowd cheered wildly as the gentlemen waved.

The air rang with the vibrant music of the Tipton General Marching Band, a twenty-piece ensemble that had the heart of a company five times its size. Flutes, trumpets, drums, and cymbals played and crashed along to the tune of John Philips Sousa's new song, "The Gladiator March." Every heart swelled with pride and joy.

The parade also included former soldiers, walking sedately. It was a day made for goodwill, and men who had fought against one other in the recent war now walked alongside each other in respectful dignity.

The fire brigade came next, and following them were the children on horseback, and then the cowboys. The more daring among them stood on their beasts, or performed tricks like rolling underneath the belly of the horse mid-stride.

It was a wonderful parade. When the last of it passed, Melinda looked to Becky and was happy to see tears that matched her own.

Merle Lacy had joined the girls, and the three spent many happy minutes recounting their favorite moments of the parade, before Becky shouted out, "Oh my! The desserts! We have to fetch them to the food site!" She grabbed Mindy by the hand and dragged her down the road and to her house. Inside, they quickly grabbed baskets stacked full of pies and cakes and hurried off again.

*

As they were setting up tables for the food, Lucas walked up. "I've been looking for you all morning, Mindy! I should have known you'd be in the middle of the activity." He looked her over and smiled. "You look ravishing!"

Mindy blushed. For once in her life, she did feel pretty. She knew it was partly the contagious mood of the day, but she was enjoying the heady sensation.

"And you look handsome yourself," she replied honestly. Lucas wore a blue suit that played against his blond hair and good looks in an altogether pleasing way. "Did you enjoy the parade?"

"I didn't watch it. I can't stand all that noise, and crowds bother me. I slept in this morning! First time I've done that in I don't know how long."

Mindy couldn't imagine how anyone could choose to stay inside on a day like this, but she had to admit, Lucas looked well rested. She remembered with a start that it hadn't been so long ago that he'd been shot. "You look like you're feeling well."

"I feel great. Let's do something!"

Mindy laughed. "Like what?"

"Let's go sign up for the games. We can do the egg toss and the frog toss together."

"I'd still like to see you sign up for that greased pig contest," Mindy teased.

"I've already told you, I'm leaving that foolishness to the young people. I am thinking about entering the Old Timer's race, though."

Mindy was puzzled. "But that's for men over fifty, Luke."

"Thanks for the compliment, my girl . . . I'll be fifty-three on my next birthday."

Mindy swallowed and tried to keep her mouth from dropping open. Fifty-three?

She said a quick farewell to Becky and then she and Luke headed toward the large open area designated for the games. They put their names on the list for both tosses and Luke paid the entrance fees. "Now what?" he asked.

"Let's go get a good seat for the speeches!" Mindy caught the disparaging look on Luke's face and gently chided, "It's our duty as citizens of these United States of America to participate in all the events today." Her tone carried a hint of humor, but she was serious—she wanted to experience it all!

*

After the speeches, lunch was served. Steven Knight was pounded on the back and thanked repeatedly for donating the meat; he happily stood at a table and carved until every piece of it was eaten.

Luke and Mindy found a secluded spot near the pond, beneath the shade of a weeping willow tree to share their lunch. As he reclined on the ground afterwards, Lucas asked, "Are you having fun?"

"Yes!" Mindy exclaimed. "This day has been heaven! I can't imagine anything that would make it better." But in her heart she knew there was one thing that might improve on this day . . . the presence of a certain black-eyed Tormentor. Her eyes had kept up a continual perusal of the crowds all morning, hoping that she might spot his familiar face. She sighed, thinking that there was no telling how long his mission would take. Saying another prayer for his safety, she realized Lucas was staring at her. "What is it? Do I have pie on my face?"

"No. Your face is perfect—just like you, Mindy." Lucas took her hand and put it to his mouth, gently placing a kiss against her knuckles. The movement made her insides tremble, but not in an altogether good way. She pulled her hand away.

"What shall we do next?" she asked.

"The games will begin soon, I'm sure. Until the announcement, I'm enjoying sitting here under this big, blue sky in your company." Lucas paused. "There are still things we need to talk about, Melinda."

"I don't know, Lucas. It's still too soon."

"It's been long enough for me to know my feelings. I want you to be my wife."

Mindy looked across the pond at the wide sea of people, her thoughts tumbling inside her noggin. Was Lucas her destiny? Was she being silly and immature and horribly fickle to consider passing up the opportunity to marry such a good man? Her heart was torn in two pieces. If only. If only.

"Is it Boone?" Lucas asked. He stared at Mindy until she met his gaze.

"I don't know, Luke. I don't know," Mindy said honestly.

"He's not for you, Melinda. He's a rambler and a drifter. He lives a dangerous life, and you'd be miserable, always wondering if he would make it home. You need something much more stable than that, something that I could give you."

Mindy looked away. She heard the words, but it sounded like they came from far away.

"I saw him this morning—" Lucas began.

Mindy's head turned quickly.

"I'm sorry. I thought you knew. He's back. This is just another example of what I'm talking about. He should have said something to you." Lucas took her hand again. "He's not the man for you, Mindy. I heard he shot and killed an old woman on this trip."

Mindy gasped. "No! He wouldn't!"

"I don't know the details. But it's what I've heard."

Dropping her head, Mindy felt her spirit fall within her. "He wouldn't, Lucas. He couldn't."

Lucas shook his head. "It's time to face the truth, Melinda. He's not for you."

Mindy looked up. Tears were in her eyes. "I can't discuss this right now, Luke. Give me more time. Please." Standing, she held out her hand. "Let's get back to the games, all right?"

*

Mindy and Lucas watched the games of skill and slowly the excitement of the day eased back into her body. They laughed at the men who chased a greased pig until they thought they might split their sides. One fellow finally held the squirming animal up in his triumphant hands, and then promptly fell—splat!—backside first into a mud puddle.

The next event was the greased pole. Men paid fifty cents each to try to climb it and remove a small American flag attached to the top. When the crowd had decided that no one could possibly earn the prize, a small, barefoot boy of about nine took a turn. He shinnied up the pole like he had done it every day of his life. The audience roared their approval!

Lucas and Mindy participated in the frog toss, and she couldn't help but laugh at the folly of it all. They were each given three "frogs"—small sacks filled with dried beans—and offered the chance to throw them onto the "lily pad"—or a steel hoop—placed several feet away. Neither one ever hit their target, but they laughed themselves silly.

In the egg toss, they only made it four rounds before their egg slipped between Lucas's outstretched arms and smashed all over him. Though Mindy could tell he tried to hold his temper, Luke was not pleased to end up with egg on his face—literally. He insisted on taking a break to cool off and clean up.

*

The rest of the day followed in like manner, with the couple trailing from one event to the next, until after the rodeo, when they found themselves on a makeshift dance floor lit by dozens of oil lamps.

The band played and couples square danced the evening away. Mindy didn't know how to square dance and so she and Luke were simply observers, until a waltz played. Lucas coaxed Mindy onto the dance floor, and she was swept away with the beauty of the moment.

The stars sparkled overhead, and Melinda was in the arms of a dashing and brave man who thought of her as "ravishing." It had been a wonderful day. Suddenly, she felt eyes upon her. On the next rotation, she searched the crowd of faces at the edges of the dance floor until she found the ones she sought. Boone was back!

Only it was obvious that his eyes did not hold the same excitement she felt. Boone stared at her with those black eyes, cold as winter and dark as midnight at the moment . . . then he turned and walked away.

Mindy's heart stopped. She did a stutter-step in the middle of the waltz and tripped Lucas up. "Uh . . . oh . . . I'm terribly sorry," she said. "That was foolish of me. I lost the count."

"That's all right, Melinda. It seems I've been waiting all night for the right moment, anyway." He made a movement with his hand toward the bandstand and the music made an awkward stop. All around them the dancers paused, confused. As they looked around for answers, what they saw was Lucas Wilhite drop to one knee before the assemblage. He took Mindy's two hands in his own, stared into her eyes and said, "Melinda McCorkle, in front of all these witnesses, here on this special day, I beg you to do me the honor of becoming my bride."

The world stopped. Mindy stared down at Lucas and her brains turned to mush. She couldn't speak, couldn't think, couldn't act. In her mind, she played over the things that Lucas had told her about Boone: catching him with another woman, his having shot a woman in cold blood. The fact he hadn't looked for her today. It seemed she didn't know the man at all. For just a moment she searched the circle of faces around them. All she saw were smiles and winks. There was no tall man with serious black eyes. In that last moment, she remembered the look Boone had given her just before he had turned and walked away from the dance floor. There was no more time for dreaming.

She looked at the man waiting before her and said, "Yes, Lucas. I'll . . . " But that was all she could say. Tears trickled from her eyes and clogged her throat.

Lucas stood and swept her up into his arms, thinking her tears were ones of joy. The people around them cheered and clapped. Inside Mindy, a bit of her began to die.

And overhead, the fireworks display began.

Chapter Thirty-Eight

July 4, 1880

Dear Mother,

I need you so desperately. I have never before known a time when I so need to sink my head upon your breast. I need to feel your comforting arms go 'round me, and hear you say that all things will work out for the best.

I have news. I am to be wed. But the thought does not fill me with joy. Instead I am filled with a deep despair. I am told all brides-to-be feel this way. Is it so? Did you feel this way with Papa?

I need you near. I wish that distance did not separate us; that I could put down my pen, walk into the next room and find you there. How I long for your wisdom and advice! Too long have I been away, for I have come to doubt my own mind, my heart, my feelings. Mother, I have promised to wed one man, while I fear I love another. What am I to do?

I have never been so close to my dream, a home of my own, a husband, and children . . . oh, but wait. That cannot happen, for he prefers to remain childless. There are so many things to consider!

I know that by the time this letter finds you, my decision will have been made. How I wish time would fly!

Above all, I would wish for your prayers. I am humbly in need of them. As always, I remain,

Your loving daughter,
Melinda

*

Mindy could not sleep Sunday night. She tossed and turned,

finally giving up. She sat in a wooden chair beside the window of her hotel room and watched until the first rays of dawn crept past her pale face. She waited until the night had fully turned to day, then she walked to the blacksmith's shop and secured the use of a horse for the day. By nine o'clock, she found herself riding through town. She rejoiced for a time, finding she could at least try to blame her tears on the wind.

After a forty-five minute ride, she found herself at the Boone homestead. She pulled up in the yard and tied off her animal. Then she tentatively climbed the front porch steps and knocked on the door. When Mrs. Boone answered, she breathed a sigh of relief.

"Why, Mindy! What brings you out at such an early hour?" Mrs. Boone asked, inviting Mindy into her home.

Mindy couldn't speak. She stood like an idiot staring at Mrs. Boone until that woman, sensing her distress, opened her arms. Mindy fell into them, sobbing. When she could speak, she apologized profusely, though she never let go or looked up into the kind eyes of the woman she had come to respect so much. The fact that it was Boone's mother made it all the more difficult.

"There, there, pet," Mrs. Boone soothed. "Nothing is as bad as all that. Come with me." Mrs. Boone walked Mindy into the parlor and sat down on the couch with her. "Now then, look me in the eyes and tell me what has happened to upset you so. When I saw you yesterday, you were in a wonderful state. What — or who — has upset you?"

"I am . . . I am . . . to be wed," Mindy managed to say.

The kind lady's eyebrows rose. "This is a recent development?"

"Yes . . . only last night. Lucas asked me to marry him and I accepted. But I can't decide why I am so broken up about it. Shouldn't I be leaping with joy? Shouldn't I be . . . happy?"

"To be honest, all brides feel at times like they might be getting into more than they can handle. This may be what you're feeling." Mrs. Boone lifted Mindy's chin. "Or it may be that you have the wrong man by the tail."

Once again, Mindy collapsed into the older woman's arms.

"Is this about Gary? Has he done something to cause this anguish? If he has, I promise you I will have his head on a platter."

"No," Mindy ground out. "He has done nothing."

Mrs. Boone sighed. "Perhaps that is the problem. Men can be idiots at times, dear. My son can be one of the biggest." The older lady spoke with more force than was necessary. "Could it be possible that you have strong feelings for my son?"

Mindy nodded.

"I was afraid of that. And now he's gone."

Mindy looked up. "Gone? Where has he gone? He only just returned!"

"Things are starting to make sense now. I knew something must have happened, because he had not planned to take another assignment so quickly. But he came in last night and announced that he must be in Dodge City by the end of the week. He left this morning with the sun, riding like the devil himself was after him." She took in Mindy's swollen, exhausted eyes. "Come. Let's put you to bed. When you wake up, we can talk more."

Standing on weak legs, Mindy clung to the older woman as they walked through the house. She allowed Boone's mother to tuck her into bed with a promise to check on her in just a bit. After she left, as Mindy lay there alone in an unfamiliar room, she became aware of a scent. Horse, and man, and leather. She realized she was lying in Boone's bed. She cradled the pillow to her face and cried herself to sleep.

*

She awoke in a strange room. It was dark outside, and it took a moment for Mindy to realize exactly where she was. She would have cried all over again, but she was dry. Dry and cold and empty. There was a hole where her heart had been, and she could feel herself slowly folding into it. But somehow, during her sleep, she had made a decision. She could not marry Lucas. He deserved more, someone who cared for him and longed for his touch.

Mississippi was calling. It was time to go home.

Mindy arose from the bed, and stood for a moment wondering what to do. She could hear Mrs. Boone humming to herself in the kitchen and Melinda started that way before realizing that she could not face Boone's mother again. Instead, Mindy slipped back into the bedroom and removed a shirt that was hanging on a wall peg. Holding it to her nose, she inhaled deeply. Then without a sound, she let herself out the front door and climbed onto her waiting horse. The ride back to town and to Lucas was one of the longest of her life.

Melinda was on a stage within two days, and headed east.

Chapter Thirty-Nine

Boone was frustrated and disgusted—frustrated that he had figured Mindy all wrong, and disgusted that he had fallen in love with someone who cared for another.

As he retraced his path toward Dodge City, he had lots of time to think. Too much time. Tumbling through his mind was every scene he'd experienced with the feisty Mindy McCorkle of Mississippi. And every scene he had hoped to experience. Stupid man, he'd actually thought things might work out between them, which proved he was plumb weak north of his ears.

Only one man stood in the way: Lucas Wilhite. Boone spit off the side of his horse. The thought of Lucas and Mindy together made him curse. It would take a long time to get her out of his mind. And his heart.

He decided to look forward. He was headed into a great job opportunity. Wyatt Earp was leaving Dodge City for Chicago, and his departure left an opening for a new deputy sheriff. After their experience together, Bat Masterson had recommended Boone for the job. It would be a departure from his life of travel and random assignments, but he found the idea of settling in one place very entertaining. He also liked the idea of sheriffing for a change. It would be good experience and could lead to other opportunities down the road.

As he rode along, he remembered the last trip, and Micah, singing his lonesome songs of love. They had more meaning to him now than they had then. He tried to recall one of the songs he'd heard so many times. Soon his voice was carrying across the open plain:

You are my sunshine, my only sunshine,

You make me happy when skies are gray.
You'll never know dear, how much I love you.
Please don't take my sunshine away.

You told me once dear, you'd always love me,
And no one else would come between,
But now you left me to love another,
You have shattered all my dreams.

*

Boone moved into a local rooming house run by a widow woman named DelSorbo. He provided her with twelve dollars a week, and in return he enjoyed a furnished room and three squares a day.

He settled into his new job right away and found he liked the pace and heartbeat of Dodge City. The only real problems the deputies faced were from the area that lay to the south of the railroad tracks, where the seedier taverns, troublesome gambling houses, and brothels lay. It was not unusual to have several reports a week about shootings and fights, since guns were only allowed in that part of town.

He and Bat got along famously. As time passed, he found he could go for hours without thinking of Mindy.

Then in September, a beat-up letter arrived that turned his world upside down once again.

*

July 23, 1880
    Boone,
    I've decided to move on. Things are not the same for me since Melinda left for Mississippi. It's been a hard decision, writing you this letter, but it's one I'm hoping will ease my conscience somewhat.

I lied to you on the morning of the celebration. Mindy had not said she would be my wife at that time. I had high hopes she would say yes if I could only knock you out of the running. To tell the truth, I would have said mite near anything to have Mindy for my own. And I guess I did. I filled her head with a lot of lies about you.

But for all my efforts, it wasn't meant to be between her and me. It seems she has feelings for another cowboy. She turned me down flat on the issue of marriage.

Since she's gone, Tipton holds no interest for me. I don't care to live on the farm anymore, because of the images I had of her there with me. I find the rooms are silent and cold, and a man can go crazy living there by himself.

I started to sell the property, but got to thinking, since your family lives here, perhaps you'd like to have it. I feel it's the least I can do for the damage I've done to your good name.

I'm enclosing the title. Do with it what you will.

Sincerely,

Lucas Wilhite

*

For days afterward, Boone pondered his options. He liked his job in Dodge City, but Tipton called to him. He stewed on the matter through the rest of September and into October. As the cold winds started to blow, his thoughts turned more and more toward his hometown. By the end of October, he had turned in his resignation and was headed for home and family.

*

Mrs. Boone was in the kitchen kneading bread when she heard the front door open. She cried aloud at the sight of her son. He looked gaunt and underfed, like he hadn't been taking care of himself, and her motherly instincts kicked in right away. She dragged him into the kitchen, plopping down biscuits and sausage left from breakfast.

"How long are you here for?" she asked, studying his troubled face.

"I reckon I'm here permanent, Ma. Lucas sent me the deed to the Larby place. I'm a homeowner now."

Mrs. Boone clucked. "Well, if you ask me, it's the least he could do! Slandering your name like he's done. People here think you murdered a woman in cold blood, though I've told them they know you better than that." She went back to her bread dough, slinging it onto the counter with a bang. After a long moment, she said, "Well, the house'll need work. I'll talk to Becky, and we'll start the process of making it more presentable." She glanced up at him. "I hope you don't plan to live there by yourself."

"Huh?" Boone gazed up at his mother. "What else would I do?"

"You're a fool, Gary Boone. I never thought I'd see the day I'd think you were downright foolish and addle-headed." She slung the bread dough a last time onto the wood-block surface and then stormed out of the room.

Boone shrugged and went back to his meal. Later he started thinking about what his mother had said. Perhaps she was right. The house did need to be made more inviting. He set to work immediately.

*

Mindy McCorkle had found peace with her life. When she returned home, she was shocked and surprised to find Richard Peters waiting for her. They began keeping company, slowly at first, then more seriously. He was a good man and she felt she could be content with him. After knowing him all her life, she felt sure there were no surprises up his sleeve.

She tried to push the memories of her trip across country out of her mind. She relegated them to a compartment of her mind marked "off limits." Sometimes in the quiet of the night, she still cried, but told herself she was foolish and addle-headed.

Her mother encouraged the relationship with Richard. She was overjoyed that Mindy had a suitor and might settle down and give her more grandchildren.

In October, the Fall Festival approached. Mindy's mother tried to get her to participate in the planning of the annual event, but the thoughts of it brought back too many memories. She planned to attend and that was good enough.

She walked through the day in a haze, thinking back over the last celebration she had attended. Too many things were similar. At the greased pig event, Mindy suddenly burst out crying. She was mortified, but couldn't help herself. Richard was caught off guard and didn't know what to do.

"Mindy, what on earth is the matter?" he asked.

"It's just so sad," she said, looking on as everyone else laughed and pointed. "The poor little pig!"

Richard looked from Mindy to the pig, and shook his head. "I never saw you cry at a greased pig contest before."

"Well, I just never thought of it from the pig's side!" She turned and began to walk away. "I can't watch anymore."

Richard hurried to catch up. "That's fine, Mindy. What do you want to do now?"

What she really wanted to do was go to her room and lie down, but she didn't say that. "I guess we can walk down and take a look at the pies for the pie contest."

They spent the rest of the afternoon meandering through the events. Mindy's handkerchief came out several times. She dabbed at her eyes and then blew her nose in a most unladylike fashion.

Late in the evening, as the sun went down, the crowd moved toward the bandstand and a temporary dance floor that had been set up. Mindy watched the square dancing and sighed. Richard was at a loss as to what he could do to cheer her flagging spirits. Mindy noticed, and thought he was a dear for trying. She determined to buck up and try to enjoy the rest of the evening.

The band began a waltz and Richard asked Mindy to dance. Though it was the last thing she wanted to do, she said yes, and even offered up a smile.

As she counted the beats in her head, Mindy thought back to her last waltz and found it hard to keep the smile on her face. She told herself if only she could get through the rest of the night, tomorrow would be a better day.

As she danced, she had an odd feeling of déjà vu. She felt eyes upon her, and she searched the crowd for anyone who might be watching. As she whirled, her thoughts wandered back to the last time. Suddenly, her heart took flight. It was Boone! Somehow she knew it. Her heart lit up with her smile, her eyes sparkled. *He's here somewhere,* she told herself. She knew too well the distinct trembling sensation she got when those black eyes were upon her.

She searched the crowds surrounding the dance floor. Round and round she and Richard went, but she was no longer dancing with Richard, she was miles away.

"I'm so glad to see you've cheered up," her companion said.

Mindy nodded.

"You're feeling better?"

Mindy nodded. "Mm hmm. Much better." She didn't meet Richard's gaze, her neck twisted this way and that as she hungrily devoured the faces, searching for just one.

Then in the shadows, she saw him. Boone—*Boone!*—leaning against a tree with his arms crossed, watching her with a stony expression she couldn't read, his dark eyes following every move, his eyes roving between Mindy and her partner.

Mindy swallowed. It was just like before, the dreamy, heady sensation that he did care! Then, in a nightmare moment she had lived through before, Boone turned and walked away.

Mindy's steps faltered. Her heart skipped, and her smile fled. She and Richard stopped in the middle of the dance floor, her hand resting lightly on his left shoulder. She looked up into his face.

"I . . . I . . . lost the count," she said.

"That's all right, Mindy. Let's pick it up again right . . . here." As the hand behind her back smoothly applied pressure, Mindy looked down, not moving, subtly shaking her head.

"I can't, Richard," Mindy said.

"Can't what, Mindy? Dance? Why, you're a wonderful dancer."

"No. I can't do this. You and me. I'm sorry."

Richard's face fell, his shoulders slumped. "What is it? Did I do something?"

"No," Mindy said. "There's someone else. And if I don't hurry, he's going to get away!" She reached up and gave Richard a kiss on the cheek. "You're a good man. You deserve more. And thank you." Then, with the beginnings of a glittering smile, she was gone.

*

Boone strode to his horse, untethered it, and started to climb on.

"Boone! Wait! Stop!"

He looked up and was surprised to see Mindy running toward him with her skirts held high. She was showing much more ankle than was proper. He smiled.

"Where are you going? How long have you been here?" Mindy's words tumbled out. Now that she was before him, her insecurities raised their troublesome heads. How could he be here for her?

"I've been here all day. I've been watching you with that new man of yours. Looks like you're doing well. I just wanted to make sure you made it safely home. The road can be a dangerous place."

"Oh. You came to see about my safety?"

Boone nodded. "I worried about you being stranded somewhere by the side of the road." Then he smiled. "Though, of course, if you had that confounded bag with you, I suppose you would have been all right."

Mindy looked down and blushed.

"Are you happy, Mindy? That's all I need to know. Are you happy here . . . with . . . him?"

Mindy looked up into Boone's black eyes. She knew her only true chance for happiness lay inside the circle of his arms. "No, Boone. I'm not happy. I haven't been happy since the day you walked away."

Boone's eyebrows rose. "Me?"

"Yes, you. You torment me beyond imagination when you're with me . . . but you torment me so much more when you're gone."

Boone lips creased into a broad smile. "Well, that's right funny. There's a little green-eyed girl that torments my thoughts as well."

He stepped closer. The moonlight washed over them, bathing the scene in soft light. He reached up a calloused hand and touched her face. "I love you, Mindy McCorkle."

"Oh!" Mindy threw her arms around him, not caring at all about propriety.

Then Boone kissed her and all became right with the world.

*

The wedding occurred a week later and took place immediately following the Sunday morning church services. Mindy wore a light pink blouse with a round neckline and a brown skirt. She carried a bouquet of yellow and pink dahlia and white baby's breath. Her niece, Sophie, skipped along before her, dropping yellow flower petals into the aisle.

Boone looked like a new man in a black cutaway suit, with a white shirt. He was freshly shaved and cologned and his smile could have lit a hundred homes in the dead of night.

Mindy's mother cried. Not only to see her last daughter wed and happy, but because Mindy was leaving. Joyous tears mixed with sad ones.

The couple traveled back to Tipton, reminiscing over the last trip. Mindy glowed with happiness, and Boone's chest stuck out in an unnatural manner. They discussed children and church and discipline and plans for the future. They fought a lot, but smiled even more.

When they arrived in Tipton, Becky and Mrs. Boone hosted a grand homecoming and wedding party for them. They were showered with good wishes and given a grand Pounding. After the party, they had enough food staples to last a year! They had been given pounds of flour, meal, eggs, coffee, and much more.

They spent the first two nights with Mrs. Boone, who promised that the Larby place had been cleaned and organized.

On the morning they rose to head to their new home, Mrs. Boone cooked a big breakfast and said, "Now you'll have to feed him well in the mornings, Mindy. He's gruff as a bear if he doesn't have his breakfast."

Mindy smiled and looked shyly at Boone. "Yes, ma'am. Thank you. That could explain a lot."

Boone laughed and took her hand. "I can't wait to get you home," he said.

"Home." Mindy spoke the word thoughtfully. "Home. I'm ready whenever you are!"

They had to borrow Becky's wagon to carry all their gifts. The trip to their new home passed in a blur of conversation.

"You know, I've been there for a while without you," Boone said, nudging Mindy with his broad shoulder. "Though I always hoped you would join me some day. I'm warning you, there are some changes since the last time you saw the place."

"Oh, Boone. No! It was perfect the way it was!"

"Well, maybe it will be more perfect. We'll have to wait and see." Boone grinned.

"What are you up to?" Mindy asked.

"Wait and see . . . "

They passed the turnoff to the property, where a large boulder lay at the foot of the drive, and Boone turned the wagon along the rutted dirt road.

"Why, everything looks the exact same, Boone! You had me worried for nothing."

They stopped: Boone climbed down and set Mindy out of the wagon. She stood in the front yard of her new home and sighed, with her hands on her hips.

"Home," Mindy said. "I like the sound of that." She turned to her new husband. "I'm happy, Boone. Really, really happy."

They began unloading the wagon and made the first trip into the house. Inside, Mindy ran her fingers over the furniture and fixtures, then whirled to Boone, "I couldn't *be* happier!" Her face was radiant.

Boone stepped over and picked Mindy up. He whirled her in a wonderful, dizzying circle and then hugged her to him. "No more tears?"

"Not anymore."

"I love you, wife."

"I love you, too, Torment."

As she glanced around the house, something out the back window caught her eye. She stepped closer to take a look and then exclaimed, "Boone! What on earth have you done?"

The pair of them stepped out the back door of the house and stood in the dirt yard. Mindy stared up at the most elaborate tree house she had ever seen. There were three levels with gradually rising stairs between.

"It's for you, Mindy." Boone said. "I built it for you. I hoped you'd come home with me some day."

"A tree house, Boone?"

Boone looked down. His face had turned a bright cherry apple red. "When I first met you, Mindy, you said you'd never been kissed, never been married, and never climbed a tree." He looked at her. "I wanted to be the one who made all those things come true."

With a cry of delight, Mindy jumped into his arms, and they whirled. Standing in the back yard of their home, while the joyous sun shone overhead, Mindy knew all her dreams had come true.

About the Author

Robyn Corum is a happy housewife and mom who lives in Hartselle, Alabama with her husband, three children, one son-in-law, one dog, one cat, and recently, two scorpions. She loves reading, crafting, creating graphics and writing. Her favorite hobbies are hunting for four-leaf clovers, gently torturing her teenagers, and celebrating when a string of words bang against each other in an altogether remarkable way.

She is author of the book, *Pieces of Her Mind*, a collection of Japanese short form poetry, with seventeen other women, available November 2012.

Robyn is currently at work on a novel about a mail order bride who is forced to leave New York City for the west in the late 1800s. Both are called "Ama."

Learn more about her at:

www.facebook.com/MelindaHeadsWest
http://about.me/robyncorum
http://pinterest.com/robyncorum

Contact her at:

robyncorum@aol.com

In the mood for more Crimson Romance? Check out *Katie's Hero* by Cody Young at *CrimsonRomance.com*.